ISBN 978-1-4303-2481-2

Published by Daudistel Publishing.

This book can be purchased at:
http://www.merrythemanofyourdreams.org

The author can be contacted at:

jadebrode@marrythemanofyourdreams.org

First Edition

When a woman changes her actions, she changes the way she sees herself.

When she changes the way she sees herself, she changes the impression she makes on others.

When she changes the impression she makes on others, she changes the caliber of men she attracts.

When she changes the caliber of men she attracts, she changes her life.

His eyes alone devour my soul, his hair, his skin, his smile, the breath he breathes is my own breath, please let me stop a while.

CONTENTS

An Introduction

There are women reading this book — and you may be one of them — who will decide the book focuses too much on manipulation without teaching women how to keep a man's love, once they have gotten him.

The truth is this. If the instructions in the book are taken seriously, and carefully put into practice, changes will take place that almost guarantee love and devotion from men of value. This book is not a stop-gap-measure for hooking men. It is about becoming a woman that men can trust!

Why would a woman go to the trouble of creating a new persona — only to revert back to her old self-serving ways which never worked in the first place? She wouldn't! Nor would a sane woman revert back to old sexual behaviors, once she discovers the kind of satisfaction that comes from temporarily delaying sexual gratification.

However…I am the first to admit that saving sex until last is a tough assignment. Most men are skilled at convincing women that instant sex is not only desirable, but also necessary if adoration is to last. How many times have we all experienced this bit of nonsense?

If you keep an open mind as you read, you will discover that the basic premise here is not about manipulating men, but about how to change your own life. And, as a result, you will attract the kind of man you have been dreaming of, and you will discover what it is like to be cherished and adored by men of value.

If you are desperately unhappy, because you don't have a great man in your life, or some man has just walked out on you, I know exactly how you are feeling.

I woke up one morning years ago and felt my life was over. The man I was in love with had left me for another woman. I couldn't decide if I wanted to scream, run away, spend the rest of my life crying, or jump off a four-story building.

But I knew I had to stop the pain. Maybe I should drive my car off a freeway overpass!

When, hysterically, I called my dearest friend and threatened to kill myself, she stopped me short. "Jade! If you kill yourself, you will erase your pain, and place it on the shoulders of your children."

So there I was, stuck with my unbearable anguish.

But I'm not in anguish any more. Today, I am a happily married woman, and I have been pretty much pain-free for the last thirty-five years. In fact, today, I don't know a woman who has the life that I have.

I paid my dues.

I want to stress that I paid my dues. My present life didn't come without effort. But the good news is that all women — every woman — can have what I have if she is willing to do the work.

The suggestions I was given, by the woman who became my mentor, were so simplistic that I thought them absurd.

"Make your bed every morning," she suggested.

"For god's sake, I'm contemplating suicide!"

"Make your bed first thing every morning," she repeated.

I was so depleted that I had given up on life. But I didn't have the strength to argue or resist, so I simply started making my bed every morning. Next, she told me to wash my old car once a week, and then she suggested I start balancing my checkbook at the end of each month. I did as directed.

One of the most important choices a woman will make is choosing a husband.

Soon, I discovered that I was feeling better. Ever so slowly, I regained my self-esteem. Then, suddenly and quite unexpectedly, I found myself standing at the altar with the man I am married to today. Being married to this man is the best thing that had ever happened to me. We have been married thirty-five years.

The life I have today started with making my bed and following directions. If you do the things suggested in this book — as I did —

your life too will become comfortable and fulfilling, because taking the high road always brings marvelous results.

FINDING THE RIGHT MAN

This book is about making one of the most important decisions you will ever make: finding the right man. Since the man you end up with will have an incalculable impact on your life, you want to choose wisely.

The premise of the book is that women have no actual rights until after they have become a man's legal partner. So…until that time, women should act like guests, because that is what they are.

The dynamics of dating are similar to the process of becoming a partner in a law firm. When an up-and-coming young lawyer is invited to join the firm, he is just another working stiff who is expected to work his butt off. He follows the rules whether he likes them or not. When he is finally invited to become a partner in the firm, his life immediately gets appreciably better. Similarly, after graduation from medical school, a young intern spends years working long hours, receiving minimal pay and even less recognition. Then one day, he becomes a certified physician. From that day forward, he is a man of power and privilege.

I implore you to view dating as a similar work project, because marriage to the right man is a big deal. If you mix casual dating with husband-hunting, you may run the risk of missing the boat.

Until you have a commitment, think of yourself as a guest.

Too often intelligent, professionally successful women turn into simpering idiots after they fall in love. With great self-confidence, they march forward and do everything wrong. They seem to turn off the left side of their brains, the logical side that has propelled them into professional success, as they become wishy-washy, indecisive idiots.

The complexity of the dating game means that women need to maintain their equilibrium and independence, while simultaneously remembering to be charming and agreeable companions. The most successful way for a woman to accomplish this delicate feat is by remembering that she is a guest. The goal is to entice, not take over. The future years of your life will depend upon how well you do this.

For women between the ages 35 and 55, short-term courtships are an imperative. If the man you are dating hasn't made up his mind by the end of six months, you would be wise to move on. I urged the women I worked with in my practice to move forward and not linger in going-nowhere relationships.

Since women can attract only men with character and ethics similar to their own, you will want to take a good look at your own strengths and weaknesses. It is strangely true that only rarely does a man connect romantically with a woman less developed than he is.

Thus, if you are a woman with an interesting personal life and enviable ethics (the result of self-discipline), you automatically eliminate lesser men from your life. Quality men look for women with character who have substantial lives. Thus, nowhere in this book will you find discussions of designer clothes, jewelry, expensive home furnishings, plastic surgery, or top-of-the-line cosmetics.

It's not about designer clothing or cosmetics.

Remember: the sublimation of immediate satisfaction, for future gain, is the hallmark of maturity. Women who develop patience and perseverance get the prize. They walk off with the men other women want.

Take a good look, now, at the man in your life, because he is a mirror reflection of you. Are you satisfied with him? Are you flattered by the caliber of men who are attracted to you? Do you long for someone more successful? More stable? If so, you may have to clean up your own act.

Try and imagine that you have been introduced to an intriguing man, and he has asked you to have dinner with him. This man is brilliant, powerful, decent and responsible. Or…perhaps the man is an Adonis; a man who loves to ski, sail and travel; a man who makes friends easily. Someone you can talk to for hours and have fun with.

How delicious life would be if you were lucky enough to attract and marry the man of your dreams. I can hear you saying, "I've never even met the kind of man I'm looking for." I understand how you feel, because I too felt that way. And, if I hadn't done the work that I am going to outline in this book, I would never have ended up with my present husband.

Walk into a life of luxury.
I was a self-centered little piece of fluff that thought mostly about herself and dated only good-looking party boys. I certainly was not the woman a successful adult man would have found interesting. Luckily, I was forced by circumstances to change. Without doing the work, I would have missed out on the life I have today.

Now if you end up with a successful executive, you would undoubtedly walk into a life of luxury. You would live in the right community, send your children to the right schools, belong to the right clubs, travel extensively and attend glamorous and exciting social functions.

If, on the other hand, you marry a sexy, masculine, outdoor type, you might live more modestly, go camping and water skiing, dress in jeans and have an exciting life with a best friend.

She was a self-centered little piece of fluff.
When I watch single women overlooking and being overlooked by potentially ideal life partners, I want to shout at them, "Stop!" I want to tell them that they too can have the life they are dreaming of....if only they will make a few changes.

The *coup d maitre* regardless of the type of man you dream of is that you must *first* work on yourself. Read this book carefully and you will become a more enticing woman. Then, when that special guy enters your life — and he will — you will sweep him off his feet. I have watched this happen to countless women as a result of doing the work.

Now just for fun …picture an elegant designer home in a gated community, or if you prefer, an attractive tract house in the suburbs. Please understand that the house you are

Do your best and watch your life change.

picturing represents your secret self. See yourself standing at the back door of the house you have chosen, knowing that the only way to get to the front of the house is by walking through the rooms.

As you walk through your house, stop in each room long enough to clean and re-organize it, keeping uppermost in your mind that the man of your dreams is waiting for you at the other end of the house, at the front door. As you work your way through the rooms of your personality, you will become a more substantial woman. Substantial women walk down the aisle with desirable men.

The pages that follow have been designed to help you correct the areas of your life that you have overlooked; in the same way you would clean your house — room by room. Do your best and watch your life change.

A Finishing School

Education

My mother was unbearably poor and she had to raise me single-handedly. Because her life was so difficult, she was determined that I should marry rich. As a result, she spent many of her leisure hours talking to me about men.

During these first four years of my life, I lived with my grandparents. My mother was employed as a nanny for one of Detroit's most socially prominent families. My uneducated mother became very familiar with the upper class and how they interacted with the world. She memorized every action and reaction of her socialite employers and when she got me back, she taught me all of the social niceties that she had been storing up in her head.

I learned because I was given no choice. My mother was a very strict disciplinarian, and she wanted me to marry rich. At the time my mother was providing me with this "finishing school" education, she simultaneously railed against God and church. As a result, I learned to hate her, because I had adored my religious grandparents. Ironically, in spite of who my mother was, and how she treated me, the things she taught me about men proved priceless.

When I was old enough to live on my own, I began applying her teachings in earnest. Consequently, I not only survived out there in the big bad world, but I managed to best most of the wealthy and sophisticated girls with whom I associated.

These tools guarantee success if you follow them.

The only time in my life that I was unsuccessful with men was the one time I deviated from my mother's teachings. I had a disastrous affair, which I will share with you later.

After recovering from what, for me, seemed like a near-death experience, I realized that I knew more about men than other women did. And although I didn't like my mother much, I had discovered that her teachings were pure gold.

FOUR BASIC RULES FOR DATING

My mother had four iron-clad, non-negotiable parental injunctions:

1) Do not chase men — never call them on the telephone.

2) Smile as often as possible — the more you smile the better.

3) Do not engage in sex — until you have a commitment.

4) Learn to listen — and make eye contact.

Never chase men. I was taught that a woman of breeding always stands still and allows men to pursue her. And, I never called men on the phone! In fact, I had

Never call men on the telephone.

been married to my now husband for over a year when one of my friends suggested I call and ask his opinion about something. I picked up our phone book and began looking for my husband's office phone number. My friend was non-pulsed. She simply could not

Smile and listen.

believe that after a year of marriage, I still did not know my own husband's phone number.

***Smile as often as possible* ...but don't flirt.** After my plunge into hopelessness, as a result of being jilted, I forgot about smiling. When this engaging activity was once again suggested by a therapist, I found it extremely difficult to do, although I had been a professional "smiler" most of my life. Slowly, I again began smiling. It was very hard at first, but it became easier the more I did it.

Save sex for last.

Sex should come last. My mother taught me that I should save sex for marriage. Today we live in a different world. Therefore, I would qualify my mother's parental injunction with save sex until after you have a commitment.   I know this sounds old-fashioned, but I also know it works.

Learn to listen. Listening requires little effort but the rewards are tremendous. A woman who makes eye contact while listening becomes a spellbinder without saying a word. Listening is the divining rod that leads to a man's soul.

Listen well.

PERSONAL POWER

While changing your behavior patterns, you may encounter periods when nothing seems to be happening. Be patient. Making changes takes time, not to mention courage and dedication.

If, tonight, the most intimate details of your life were to be aired on the six o'clock news, how would you feel? Would you be delighted?

Would you invite your neighbors over to watch? If your answer to this question is "No, not really," you probably have work to do.

Are you aware that every action you take and every word that you speak determines the outcome of your life? Too often, women think that they can "get away with" the things they do behind closed doors. But, I am convinced that every action we take comes back to us. However, the results of our actions do not always return immediately. Sometimes it takes years. The tricky part is this *time* factor.

I may do something sneaky, downright dishonest or horrifically immoral, and seemingly not have to pay a price. But years later, my actions and selfishness will return to haunt me. This time lapse often makes the concept difficult to grasp.

Do women really think they can get away with it?

I have spent hours talking with men, including ex-convicts. Inmates have a saying: "What goes 'round comes 'round."

We sometimes tell ourselves only the things we want to hear. We convince ourselves that our private lives are our own affair. "I can do whatever I want to do. No one is going to control me! Anyway, no one needs to know how many men I sleep with."

But reality usually proves us wrong, because the one person we can't outsmart is ourselves. The self always knows, and we then become our own judge and jury.

A highly developed older man once told me that life is like a steel rod, no one can bend or break it, no matter how rich or powerful or smart. "No one can," he said, "outwit the law of cause and effect." He went on to explain that this law works in things both big and small. It is all inclusive.

This goes from not making one's bed in the morning to sleeping with another woman's husband...from neglecting to make credit card payments to declaring bankruptcy...from stealing medicine from someone's medicine chest to dealing hard drugs...from self-centeredness to self-destruction.

For instance, when a woman vacuums her carpet, she sees immediate results. But the consequences of secret actions are not always so self-evident. Women often assume they have gotten away with their little "indiscretions," when the sad truth is that every action — good or bad — eventually returns to us.

Let's say that I am on a diet and I sneak a piece of chocolate cake. After eating the cake, nothing happens, so I decide to have a small piece of apple pie. Again nothing happens. For several more weeks, I sneak deserts now and then. Nothing seems to happen.

I smile to myself. I have outwitted the system!

Then, one day, I have a date with a gorgeous man — a man I want to impress. I take out my best pair of black slacks — the ones that make me look so slim and trim — and horrors! They're too tight!

Similarly, a woman can have sex with scores of different men and seemingly not pay a price. But years later, she usually looks harder and tougher than her more discrete sisters.

Men have two ways of relating to women.

Sharp personality edges and hardened facial expressions are the price women pay for their cavalier sexual indulgences.

Men seem to have two ways of relating to women: overly protective or challenging and combative. It's a man thing! And sex without prior commitment does not engender protectiveness from men.

Without commitment before sex, men seem to take off their kid gloves and thoroughly enjoy hand-to-hand combat with the women with whom they are having sex. These encounters become a fun challenge, as he asks himself how much sex he can get without anteing up. For less than scrupulous men, this kind of gamesmanship is addictive, because it is ego inflating.

Commanding men, man-to-man, are rough and tough. They can be brutally frank. When a woman is on the receiving end of this kind of interchange from men, it hardens her. Men save their gentler side for the women with whom they have fallen in love. Men of value do not usually fall in love with women who are cavalier about sex.

When dating, you are the one in charge of the evening.

When on a date, do you understand that ultimately it is you — and not he — that is in charge of the evening? Yes, indeed! You can be in control if you want to be. Society tries to convince women that it is men who have the power. Not true! The person who holds the power is the person with the final word. Women have the final word!

Are you aware that the poor guys risk rejection every time they invite or call a woman? They must drive, pay for the evening, open doors and make reservations, but it is we women who get the final say: "yes" or "no."

And now…the big question: how can you find the right man? This question is similar to asking, "Why does God allow sickness?" The answer to these questions is unknown. Even so, there does seem to be order in the world in which we live.

Wasn't Aristotle one of the first to define the law of cause and effect? Ralph Waldo Emerson's Law of Compensation said much the same thing: action and reaction are a vital part of nature and every act finds its own reward.

HIGH SELF-ESTEEM

My own self-esteem disappeared after a collapsed love affair which just about carried me off into another dimension. A gigolo named Peter swept into my life and wooed me with seemingly selfless devotion and adoration.

When Peter walked out of my life with no warning, I split into a million pieces. I became completely non-functioning. I couldn't sleep. I had no interest in life! I had no energy and it seemed no reason for living, although I had three school age children.

The most fulfilling life she could ever have imagined.

As I would awaken each morning, I couldn't bear the thought of facing another day. In the first few weeks, I would pray for God to take me home. I thought about killing myself, but I didn't have the courage.

During these on-going weeks of anguish, no one could have convinced me that the greatest life I could ever imagine lay just before me. My new life was only nine months away, but as it crept along it seemed more like fifteen years. Those tough months changed my life. In retrospect, I understand that the worst days of my life were actually the beginning of the best years of my life.

I had always thought of myself as a basically decent person. I didn't lie (maybe I exaggerated a little). I didn't steal (although I didn't try to return money I found or correct someone who made change in my favor). And I hadn't killed anyone (not physically at least).

Therefore, I thought of myself as a decent person who had survived a difficult childhood. The truth of the matter was that I was an iron fist in a velvet glove. And everything was always about *me*.

THE RIGHT MAN

Some of the women who came to see me—I'm a psychotherapist—thought of dating as an answer to loneliness. And most of these women were convinced that sex early-on was mandatory if they expected a man to return. They seemed to think they were not "enough" unless they agreed to sex.

My clients were attractive, physically fit and doing well professionally, but they were all depressed because they were not attracting, and keeping, the kind of men they wanted. And they asked the same questions: Why did he stop calling? What made him lose interest? What did I do wrong?

Winning is always hard work.

Women usually scheduled an appointment with me only after several broken love affairs. So, if you are a woman who hasn't yet put it together with the right man, now may be the time to take stock.

Winning the heart of a man of value is hard work. But careful attention to detail will bring delightful results.

A TWO-CARAT DIAMOND RING

Imagine that you are the owner of a near-flawless blue-white two-carat diamond ring. If you owned such a ring, how carefully would you take care of it?

As you washed your hands in a public restroom would you lay your ring on the counter? Would you casually slip it off your finger when an acquaintance asked to try it on?

Would you leave it in your hotel room when you went for a swim or a massage? On the other hand, if you owned an inexpensive, two-carat cubic zirconium? How much thought would you give to taking care of that ring? Would you be as careful with it as you would be with your two-carat diamond?

Think of dating as a job interview.

Obviously not. Although these two rings are similar in appearance, they have very different values. So it is with women.

THE WOMEN MEN CAN'T RESIST

When a woman knows in her heart-of-hearts that her life is in order, that her friends are of the highest caliber, her bills are paid, her house is well kept and she is behaving responsibly in most areas of her life, she reflects this in the way she walks and talks. Then...she attracts the right man. The way men respond is pretty much a reflection of how a woman perceives herself.

In addition to the few men I worked with professionally, I have talked with dozens of other men over the years. Men seem to be unanimous in their hope that the woman they are attracted to as possible life partners will have sufficient self-esteem to hold off on sex, even as they try to convince her not to.

Men: rich or poor, educated or uneducated, good looking or not so good looking, sophisticated, blue-collared or

Men of substance view life differently.

brainiacs — are all looking for women with high self-esteem. Men want women who are responsible, trustworthy and nurturing. And, since the ratio of women to men is disparate, high quality men have a reasonable chance of getting exactly the kind of woman they want.

If you will address yourself to the issues raised in this book, you will become a man magnet. And then you can write your own ticket.

My assignment, as I see it, is to help *you* become the special woman decent men dream of finding.

It is important to remember that after a man reaches maturity, there is more to capturing his heart than beauty and sex. A successful plan for the woman who wants to be married is to think of dating as similar to a job interview, rather than thinking of it as an evening's entertainment.

Most attractive and well-established men have scores of women chasing after them. And these women are usually more-than-willing to engage in immediate sex—or sex after one or two dates. But, it takes more than instant sexual gratification to hook a man of value, after he has reached a certain age.

I have watched women turn their lives around as a result of the simple suggestions in this book. The bright and talented women I saw in my practice had been going from one disastrous affair into another. After working with them, I was delighted to watch them move into solid and rewarding relationships and marriages.

Become a woman of value or not, as you choose.

ARE YOU A KEEPER?

Are you the kind of woman a noteworthy man will have trouble resisting?

- ❖ Is your home clean and inviting?

- ❖ Are your children well cared for?

- ❖ Do you read the newspaper or listen to the news every day?

- ❖ Do you lock your doors and draw your drapes at night?

- ❖ Do you have a respectable savings account?

- ❖ Do you dress conservatively?

- ❖ Are you aware that less-is-more when it comes to make-up?

- ❖ Do you refrain from using expletives, at least in public?

- ❖ Do you have a fulfilling social life?

- ❖ Do you drink only in moderation when dating?

- ❖ Do you make sure that sex is the last thing on your dating agenda?

If you answered yes to these questions you get an "A".

CATCHING A BIG FISH

I think husband-hunting and trout-fishing are similar. For instance, a good fisherman takes himself to a stream where he thinks the fish are biting, attaches a lure to his line, casts out his line and waits.

He knows the importance of patience.

When a good fisherman feels a tug on his line, he reels in very slowly. The bigger the fish, the more slowly the fisherman reels in. Only after the catch is safely in his net, does the expert fisherman relax.

A woman hoping to marry an outstanding man will do well to emulate the competent fisherman. And, indeed, some do!

When a savvy and sophisticated woman finds herself in the presence of a man to whom she is attracted – and feels that tug on her heart we all know so well – she doesn't shift into high gear.

Oh, no! On the contrary, the disciplined woman carefully monitors herself. She smiles and briefly invites with her eyes, but nothing more.

Clever and knowledgeable women know the importance of holding back. They, like the skilled fisherman, are adept at the art of patience. The sophisticated woman knows that the more elusive she appears, the more desirable she becomes.

IT'S NEVER TOO LATE TO START OVER

The woman in this story had an enviable Ivy League education. As a young woman she was a beauty. Most of her life she excelled at everything she undertook.

She was a virgin when she married, and during her marriage, she was sure she had missed out on something important. So, when the marriage ended in divorce, she set out to

It is never too late.

discover what she had been missing.

At breakneck speed, listening to no one, she proceeded from one unsuccessful affair to the next. Finally, after ten years of heartbreak, she has stopped dating.

She said this: "I always considered myself to be hip, slick and cool; smart, sexy, and attractive. But you, Jade, kept telling me that I was doing things wrong and kept citing your damn law of cause and effect. But not me! Oh no, I'm a free spirit, I said. I don't have to live by those rules. Still…I just couldn't get it right.

"Now, here I am in my so-called mature years, and well, I'm alone. What else can I say except that maybe it's not too late even for me?"

Of course it's not too late. It is never too late. Small changes have dramatic effect and make a big difference.

STROLLING INTO THE WEST WING

I was young and gullible and my first husband had convinced me that only one man could win the upcoming election. That man was Richard Nixon. According to my husband, Nixon was definitely going to be our next president.

When my husband invited me to go to Washington, D.C. with him on a business trip, I was thrilled. He told me he would talk to his parents, who were friends of Senator Henry Jackson, and see if the Senator could arrange a personal introduction to Vice President Nixon.

Two days later, we were on a plane for Washington D.C., but when we arrived, I discovered that the vice president had been called out of town. I was so disappointed I almost cried.

I finally consoled myself by getting tickets for a tour of the White House. This was a scary undertaking for me to take on. I had lived a very sheltered life and I was not accustomed to venturing out by myself.

The following morning, after my husband left for work, I took a deep breath and readied myself for the challenging day ahead of me. I chose what I was going to wear very carefully, deciding on a pale blue cashmere suit, black calfskin heels and wrist-length kid gloves, which back then were a necessity for women of refinement. When I had finished dressing, I examined myself in the mirror and was pleased with my own reflection.

I arrived at the East Gate in time for the first tour of the day and, although I was only half-heartedly interested in the history of the White House, I was proud of myself to be doing something of this magnitude alone.

I was also depressed. I had so much wanted to meet Vice President Nixon.

After our tour began, we stopped to listen to a docent explain something – I don't know what since I wasn't paying attention – when an announcement came over the loudspeaker saying that the vice president's helicopter had just landed on the South Lawn!

I felt an instant rush.

At the time of the announcement, my group happened to be standing in front of a bright yellow rope which was restricting entrance to a long white marble hallway. It had just been explained to us that this corridor leading to the West Wing.

As the docent droned on and on, I remember looking down the long hallway, and seeing at about fifty-foot intervals, three serious-looking men in dark suits, each standing with his back to the wall. It took only a few seconds to conclude they were Secret Service.

As my tour group began to move on, something inside of me snapped. And before I knew what was happening, I found I had slipped underneath the yellow rope, and was striding full-tilt down the long marble corridor.

"What in the world are you doing?" I asked myself, but I kept on walking. Passing the first Secret Service man, I smiled, and said, "I'm looking for the office of the vice president." Just as if I knew exactly what I was about.

I was beginning to perspire.

The serious-looking man standing against the wall must have assumed I was a member of the press, because he motioned me forward, adding in a very firm voice, "Please, put on your press badge!"

His no-nonsense manner terrified me, but I continued walking.

When I passed the second Secret Service man, he simply looked back at the first man, and inclining his head forward, indicated that I should continue. The third Agent barely acknowledged my existence.

Arriving at the end of the corridor, I found myself entering a small room filled to the brim with people, all of whom were talking all at once. The noise level was numbing. Then I noticed that everyone was wearing a badge.

I was standing among the press!

Inside the doorway of this jam-packed room, an officious looking older woman sat behind a large imposing desk. She indifferently acknowledged my presence and returned to whatever she was doing.

I began to shake.

I knew that I was in way over my head. But I couldn't think of a way to extricate myself. So, being young and foolish, I took a deep breath and continued on my way. In spite of my terror—and terror is the right word—I was determined to meet the vice president.

Next, I found myself standing in front of yet another imposing desk. This desk, however, was commanded by a no-nonsense woman. She stopped me cold!

"May I help you?" she demanded in a mean autocratic voice.

As if I knew exactly who I was, I calmly replied, "I'm here to see the vice president." To this day, I have no idea how I managed to keep from throwing up.

To my further consternation, this formidable woman, simply stood up and motioned for me to follow her. She then ushered me into the office of the vice president of the United States!

At this point, my mind and body seemed to separate. I still knew who I was, but I couldn't connect with myself. The ringing in my ears was deafening. Before I could think of a reasonable resolution, I heard an explosion of heavy footsteps, accompanied by a flutter of added activity.

The Vice President of the United States.

Next thing I knew, two very serious men (obviously Secret Service) had entered the vice president's Office and were standing on either side of me.

I froze!

From the outer office, I could now hear a woman's voice telling *someone* that a young woman was waiting to see the vice president.

After that everything happened so fast.

Suddenly…the vice president of the United States was walking through the door of his office with a broad smile on his face and his right hand extended.

"Oh, my God! I'm going to faint."

But, willing myself not to pass out, I extended my hand and introduce myself.

"My name is Jade Jenks," I said. "It is a pleasure to meet you, Mr. Nixon." And with that, I smiled my best smile and turned, and walked out of the office of the vice president of the United States. And no one tried to stop me.

Telling myself not to run, I made my way down the inner hallway, through the room filled with the press out of the West Wing and down the long marble corridor.

I told myself to walk slowly. I remembered to keep my shoulders back, hold head high and look straight ahead. After what seemed like an eternity, I slipped under the yellow rope, and melded into an oncoming tour group.

This is a true story. I think it demonstrates that women are often more capable than they give themselves credit for. Perhaps you, too, are under estimating yourself.

ENTERING THE GATES OF HELL

J ust prior to graduation from the University of Washington, I foolishly
quit school to marry a fraternity boy. My fiancé was a Bostonian: well
bred, good-looking, ambitious and from a prominent Back Bay
family. Definitely a catch! Everyone assumed that only good fortune
awaited me.

Indeed, within only a few years, my young husband and I were well on our way up the ladder of success. We had joined the right clubs, drove the right cars, wore the right clothes, made friends with all the right people, and had three bright, sparkling, children— who dared not misbehave.

As time wore on, however, my impressive young husband became distant and pre-occupied, driving himself relentlessly and insisting that I do likewise. With no interest in doing so, I joined the Junior League. I then associated exclusively with sophisticated and intimidating women with whom I had little in common.

Did good fortune really await them?

As my husband pushed himself harder and harder in his quest for fame and fortune, he developed a taste for martini lunches, afternoon golf – and other women. I tried desperately to keep our marriage together, but the harder I tried, the more impossible things became. I felt like a diamond-studded wrist watch that my husband enjoyed showing off, but otherwise didn't have time for. Soon, I became a physical and an emotional wreck: I smoked excessively, took pills and started losing weight.

She was an emotional wreck.

When my husband (who was the boss of everything!) decided that I was neglecting my responsibilities, he told me to get professional help. Dutifully, I began seeing a psychiatrist three times a week. During my sessions, I did nothing but complain about my husband and my marriage.

During one session, which turned out to be my last, the psychiatrist stared at me for a long time without saying a word. Finally, in a very serious voice, he said, "The only difference between you and a professional call girl, Jade, is price."

I was shocked into dead silence.

Seemingly oblivious, he continued, "Your price is: marriage, a large house, designer clothes and jewelry."

Smirking, he added, "I doubt that you are worth it."

I wanted to kill him!

Instead, I sat in stone-cold silence and glared at him. Then, without another word, I rose from my chair and stalked out of his office. Driving back to our house, I was blinded by tears of fury and frustration.

I'm filing for divorce.

As soon as I arrived home, I marched purposefully into the living room, where my husband sat reading the paper, and announced at the top of my lungs, "I'm filing for a divorce!"

My husband looked at me as if I had lost my mind. But I wasn't kidding; the next day, I saw a lawyer and started divorce proceedings.

In retrospect, I think my psychiatrist was very skilled. He made me so angry that my fury overcame my fear, and I was able to walk away from a destructive thirteen-year marriage.

Immediately, I began to feel better. I was now ready to throw off the shackles that had been binding me and go out and have fun. I was thirty-four years old, and I could hardly wait for moonlight, romance and roses.

I was still attractive, and like so many young women with good bodies and a pretty face, I assumed that success with men was something I would always be able to count on.

How wrong I was!

After the divorce was final, my ex-husband bought a lovely three-bedroom house near the ocean, and told me that the children and I could live in this house rent-free. (He wanted *his* children to grow up in the right community.)

There was one tiny condition. My ex had obtained a court order which stated that *only* his three children, a dog named Snoopy and cat named Digit (and as an afterthought) – I – were to occupy his house for any period lasting longer than four hours.

Although his stipulations were humiliating, things still went along smoothly for more than a year.

Then I met Peter.

A friend introduced me to Peter at a cocktail party. Peter was Hollywood gorgeous. He was also quick-witted, broad-shouldered and in prime physical condition. He was also emotionally open and vulnerable, almost like another woman, and I found him absolutely enthralling after my cold, controlling ex-husband.

Peter was ten years younger.

Peter was also ten years my junior.

As the cocktail party began winding down, Peter asked if I would like to go somewhere and have a cup of coffee. Was he kidding? Of course! I would love to go somewhere and have coffee with him. Before I had finished my first cup of coffee, I was in love.

We began seeing each other twice a week and Peter doted on me. He would drive to my house, pick me up, and then drive back to his apartment where he would cook marvelous gourmet meals for us.

After our romantic candlelight dinners, Peter would draw my bath, pour expensive bubble bath in the tub, and put lighted candles about. As I luxuriated in the warm sudsy water, Peter would serenade me. He had a magnificent baritone voice.

Peter would tell me, over and over again, that I was the most beautiful woman he had ever known. After thirteen years of marriage, to what I referred to as a stuffed shirt, I was overwhelmed by his attention and adoration.

Our love affair lasted for eighteen months.

The affair lasted eighteen months.

As things began to unravel, I sensed that something was wrong, but couldn't quite identify it. Then one day – from out of nowhere – Peter announced that he was leaving me for another woman!

I shut down completely. The room started reeling, my vision blurred and I felt like I was on fire. And I cried. I couldn't sleep, I couldn't eat. I thought about suicide. This went on for several weeks.

Finally, my ex-husband picked up on what he termed "more of your mother's erratic behavior" and started pinning the children down with questions. Up to this point, my ex had more-or-less dismissed Peter as being inconsequential. But now, as he watched me losing it, he became aggressively angry and agitated.

She wanted to push him off a cliff.

Several days later, he sent me a registered letter saying that I (which, incidentally, included his children) could no longer live in *his* house. He gave me two weeks in which to move. To add insult to injury, he immediately stopped making his child support payments.

I wanted to push him off a cliff! Unfortunately, I didn't have the emotional strength needed to confront him.

I simply accepted his edict. We had to move.

Since I have no relatives that I could turn to, and I had no savings, I vaulted from sorrow into extreme panic. But eventually, I was able to pull myself together, and I went apartment hunting. I was able to find a dingy, two-bedroom apartment with a small wood-burning fireplace.

The prospect of moving was beyond my scope – absolutely overwhelming! And, believe this or not, it was only after I had signed a year's lease on the tiny, run-down apartment, that I realized I had rented something *too small* to accommodate my large custom made furnishings.

I solved this problem by *giving away* my magnificent furnishings. Although I had only pocket change left from my divorce settlement, it did not occur to me to sell my things. I was in the middle of what I would now describe as a walking nervous breakdown. But there was no responsible person to step up and take over, so I did what so many street people do: I walked around mindlessly.

Their new home was now complete.

Two weeks later, with the help of friends, I moved into the dreadful little apartment. The move itself was not difficult, because there wasn't much left to move. And, it was only after my friends had hugged me and said goodbye that I realized I had given away some very essential household items. In addition to most of my furniture, I had also given away the kitchen table and my king-size bed.

I sat down and cried! Actually I collapsed on the floor and sobbed.

Afterward, with the most overwhelming sense of shame, I gathered up my children and drove to the local Salvation Army Thrift Shop. There, I found a dilapidated dark green couch, a card table with four mismatched chairs – the substitute for a kitchen table – a queen-size mattress which they assured me had been fumigated, several strange-looking lamps and three large and ornate picture frames. (My ex had already helped himself to our exquisite oil paintings.)

I had, for some inexplicable reason, saved my good linens, my sterling flatware and my china and crystal. Apparently, in spite of an overwhelming desire to self-destruct, I still maintained some vestige of self-esteem. I think my elegant linens and tableware gave me hope.

For the next several months, each morning upon awakening, I would vow that "someday" I would again have the lifestyle I had lost. But for now, there were more immediate problems.

We had no dressers for our clothes and there was no more money.

I have always been resourceful, so, with my children once again in tow, I drove to our local market to look for orange crates. (Oranges were shipped in wooden crates back in those days.) The men who worked at the market must have sensed my desperation, because they found several near-perfect orange crates for us.

These became our dressers. The days wore on …

When I snapped out of my depression, I became acutely aware of how dismal the apartment was and how badly it needed paint. I went to a hardware store and bought three gallons of white paint and a pint of yellow paint. And I started painting.

I painted the bathroom, the kitchen cupboards, the closet doors and the orange crates. I painted everything white, except the ornate picture frames, which I painted yellow. When the picture frames were dry, I hung the empty frames on the wall above the old couch. "I'll find something to put in them later," I told myself.

One of my friends gave us a beautiful hand-knit afghan as a house-warming present, and I draped this over the old couch. Another friend gave us several large indoor hanging plants.

I was cross and cranky. I fretted endlessly about my losses. I mourned my fate. Since I was still semi-suicidal, it was easy to focus on how unfairly life had treated me. When I wanted to make myself feel really bad, I would daydream about our big house in South Pasadena. I could picture in my mind's eye this five-bedroom Tudor-style home sitting on an acre, in just the right neighborhood, with its forty-two-foot swimming pool, a tennis court and exquisitely landscaped gardens.

I drove myself crazy feeling sorry for myself!

When I finished with one destructive obsession, I would immediately slip into the next. Another way of torturing me was to recall a trip to New York that I had taken with my ex-husband before things had gotten so awful.

No husband and no hope. In New York, we had stayed on the fourteenth floor of the St. Regis Hotel in the suite, that just the night before, Richard Burton and Elizabeth Taylor had occupied. Our suite included a private maid who responded immediately to a slight pull on a long velvet cord. Luxury!

The sitting room in the suite was furnished in lovely antiques. It also had an ornate fireplace that came to life with the press of a button. The bathroom was enormous. There was a seven-foot bathtub, which could easily have accommodated a family of four.

"But now! Here I sit in this dreadful apartment with no money, no husband and no hope." My misery was beyond words. Little did I know that more misery was awaiting me.

As a child and teenager, even though we were desperately poor, I had been terribly indulged and restricted. I had never been allowed to work, not even a part-time job after school. I was never allowed to do housework! When I was a senior in high school, I still did not know how to do the dishes. My mother insisted on washing and ironing all of my clothes and laying them out for me. As I have said, my mother was rather strange.

And now. Now I had to find a full-time job in order for us to eat and pay the rent. The thought of working full-time terrified me and made me sick to my stomach.

Fortunately, when I was in college, my mother had insisted that I take typing and shorthand. This was in addition to the requirements for my major which was English literature, the perfect career choice for a young woman with no family and no money. My mother told me that the day might come I would need some practical skills to fall back on.

Thanks, Mom!

I got a job very quickly. I seem to present well even when I was half-crazed. I went to work for a local bank. The women who worked in the bank were very different

Two things that changed her life.

from the women I had associated with during my marriage. These women were down-to-earth and definitely living in the fast lane. I soon became a part of their group.

We drank together, we partied together and we talked endlessly about men.

I was having the time of my life. It never crossed my mind there might be consequences. Then, two things happened that were to change my life. The first took place at a local gas station.

As I drove into the station in my dirty car – the one replacing my light blue Mercedes – some ungainly, lumbering fellow dressed in a pair of old jeans and a dirty shirt, swaggered over to my car. Grinning, or rather leering at me, he began washing and re-washing my windshield. Finally, he leaned his head into the driver's window said, "If you wait around until I get off work, we can go to the bar across the street and have a drink."

I was speechless!

It was a sobering moment.

The next incident was even more humiliating. I was out on the town with the girls from my office, and as usual, we were looking for excitement. For lack of something better to do, we decided to go to the Santa Monica Pier where a temporary amusement park was in full swing.

Once there, our attention was immediately drawn to a two-story-high slide. We watched people laughing and screaming as they slid down the slide on large burlap bags. We all bought tickets.

Forging ahead of my friends, I began climbing the stairs up to the top of the slide. But as I got near the top, I started having second

Time to knuckle down.

thoughts, and was about to turn around and go back down the stairs when a gorgeous hunk of a guy whispered in my ear, "If you're afraid to go down by yourself, I'll take you."

"Yes, thank you," I said, demurely smiling.

The bronzed and muscled Adonis sat down on a burlap sack, held out his arms invitingly, and I slipped into them. And down the slide we went! It was both fun and exhilarating. When we reached the bottom of the slide, my sexy young admirer nodded indifferently at me and proceeded to shimmy unaided back up the slide.

Without so much as a backward glance!

Since I wasn't used to this kind of indifference from men, my competitive genes roared into action, and I said to myself, "I certainly can do anything that arrogant little jerk can do."

But I was wrong!

To my utter dismay, I found I was no longer the agile little thing I thought myself to be, because no matter how hard I tried, I could not climb up that damn slide. It was a sobering moment.

Later that night, as I lay on my mattress on the floor, I kept re-living my ride down that damn slide. I could not let go of the fact that some insignificant surfer-type nobody had seen "me" as a good deed. My annoyance eventually gave way to

Any thing you can dream of — you can have.

questioning. Could the magic that had always been mine, somehow have vanished? Was I already over the hill?

I slept very little that night. But, by morning, I had gained some perspective. Actually I had an epiphany! For the first time in my life, I now understood that my failure had nothing to do with age or bad luck. The truth was far more shattering. My cavalier attitude toward responsibility had put me where I now found myself.

In fact, I decided that life was similar to my ride down that huge slide. Exhilarating and exciting going *down*, but it was oh so difficult trying to get back up.

At this point in my life, my finances were a disaster, my car was old, dilapidated and dirty, my clothes were in disarray and my children had been more or less raising themselves. At that moment, I now realized that if I was ever going to get back the life I had walked away from, I was going to have to knuckle down and get to work.

But I was clueless as to how to do this.

Trying so hard to grow up.

In desperation, I got down on my knees – something I had not done in years—and began to pray. As I was trying to pray, I remembered an article that I had read in the Los Angeles Times quoting new age guru, Tony Robbins.

"The way that I learned to shoot a gun was to find the best marksman I could find, and copy everything the guy did. The way he moved, the way he breathed, the way he held his gun." Okay!

I knew who I was going to talk to: the bank manager where I worked. She was married and she was very much in love with her husband. And this woman definitely had what I wanted. The next day, I asked her if we could get together for lunch.

Over lunch, I told this woman that I had made a mess of my life and I wanted my old lifestyle back. I said I was willing to do anything she suggested, explaining that I didn't have a mother or sister that I could turn to.

"Tell me exactly what you want," she gently said.

"I want to be married again! I want a man who is strong and dependable who will really love me. And love my children. I also want someone who is successful."

After a moment of silence I added, "I guess I want it all."

"You can have anything you can dream of, Jade. If…you are willing to work for it."

"How do I work for the right kind of man?" I whined.

"You can start by asking yourself some questions. Ask yourself what you think "he" would be doing in every circumstance in which you find yourself. Then try and pattern *your* life after the life you think he is living. If you are looking for an adult, you must first become an adult.

I didn't much care for my new mentor at that moment.

"Secondly," she continued, ignoring my petulance, "write a letter to God explaining exactly what you want. Be specific. Tell God you are willing to work hard."

I hated her! But what choice did I have?

That night I wrote the damn letter. And the next morning, I actually began asking myself how the man I longed for would be living *his* life. Actually, I knew "exactly" how he would be living.

I was immature. I wasn't stupid.

The kind of man I wanted would be doing what all responsible adults do. He would be working hard and shouldering a great deal of responsibility. I, on the other hand, had for years been avoiding all responsibility. For instance, whenever I got overdrawn notices from a bank, I simply changed banks. But now I wanted to change me. I asked one of my friends to show me how to balance my bank account, and thereafter, I balanced my own checkbook every month. No matter how long it took.

...and she began to pray.

I began washing my car every week, by myself, by hand. I scrubbed our kitchen and bathroom floors, on my knees. I washed our apartment windows, inside and out. I polished our shoes.

I also cried a lot.

The business of trying to grow up – although, at the time, I didn't know that was what I was doing – was so hard. There were moments when I felt I would die from the effort.

No such luck!

I had, always, all of my life, had dates on weekends. For me, it was a disgrace to be "at home" on a Saturday night. But dating just to be dating was so counter-productive, and it certainly hadn't gotten me where I wanted to go.

So, for the next nine months, I spent my Friday and Saturday nights at home, alone. Oh, occasionally, I would have dinner with a girlfriend. But I spent most weekends cleaning our apartment, doing the laundry, ironing my clothes, polishing my nails and being there for my children.

Throughout this dreadful period, my mentor kept assuring me that the Right Man would come along, if I continued doing the right things. I tried to stay upbeat, but deep down inside of me, I was sure the whole unholy, agonizing process was going to kill me!

Then, instead of something wonderful happening as a result of all of my hard work, I got fired from my job at the bank. "Why was this happening to me?" I moaned.

After sulking for a few days, I pulled myself together and went out looking for another job. Luckily I found something immediately. I was hired as a technical secretary to a scientific research firm in Santa Monica, and they gave me a desk in an alcove off the main hallway.

People were constantly walking by my desk, and for several months a Dr. Brode, one of the owners, passed my desk a dozen times a day, without acknowledging me. Oh, maybe a perfunctory nod or a very curt good morning. I thought him an arrogant ass.

One day, Dr. Brode stopped to talk with one of the other scientists, and thereafter this became his daily habit. Whenever he stopped in front of my desk, I would turn off my electric typewriter (we didn't have personal computers in those days) and sit quietly with my hands folded in my lap.

In the beginning, I wasn't acknowledged. But, as time wore on, I began to be included in the conversations. This went on for weeks.

It takes time and patience.

Then, one afternoon Dr. Brode did not return to work after lunch. I thought nothing of it, since I knew he played handball every day at noon. But later in the day, one of the scientists told me that he had been hit in the eye with a handball and that he might lose sight in his left eye.

My immediate reaction was to call his house to see if he was all right. As this thought crossed my mind, I could feel my body responding with a flush. And then it hit me!

"Oh my god! You have become emotionally involved with a married man!"

My mother had spent a lifetime drilling into me that married men were always off-limits. Therefore, I knew that I had to do something, and do it fast.

Good at getting jobs — not good at keeping them.

I marched myself across the street to the corporate offices, and asked for an immediate transfer. And I was given the transfer, but only because one of the scientists had been asking for a technical secretary. The head of personnel told me that I could move my things the following morning.

The next day, as I was packing up my stuff, Dr. Brode passed my desk as usual. He was wearing a patch over his right eye. Other than the patch, he seemed fine and in good spirits. When he noticed that I was clearing out my desk, he asked what I was doing.

"I'm being transferred to the building across the street," I said matter-of-factly.

He said nothing. Then, he abruptly turned and walked away. Several minutes later, he returned. In a very stern tone of voice, he said, "I need to talk to you, Jade. Let's take a walk around the block." He wasn't asking.

"Oh no," I thought, "I'm going to be fired again!"

I followed him out the front door and we began walking. At first, he rambled on about the company policy, and then he switched to the weather. I held my breath.

Suddenly, he stopped! I held my breath some more. I had no idea what was coming, but I knew it was going to be something awful.

Finally, he said in a powerful kind of voice, "I think I've fallen in love with you, Jade. Will you have dinner with me tonight?"

I think I've fallen in love with you.

I almost fainted!

My mind started going around in circles. When I could get my breath, I eked out, "I can't do that. You're a married man!"

"I'll move out," he calmly replied, as he continued staring at me with a look of quiet resolve.

Now…I thought he meant that he was going to "move out" and file for divorce. Silly me!

Thinking that he would be moving into a hotel, I agreed to have dinner with him.

Later that evening, when Len – I couldn't keep calling him Dr. Brode could I? – came to pick me up, he must have found our little apartment very... uh... interesting. But being the gentleman that he is, he acted as though "large-picture-frames-minus-pictures" were nothing out of the ordinary. (I had not yet accumulated enough extra to buy pictures for the empty frames.)

Mr. Wonderful simply smiled and helped me on with my jacket.

We drove to a quaint little French restaurant in Santa Monica and had a delightful evening. He was so smart, so powerful and sure of himself that he made me feel utterly and perfectly safe.

As we were driving back to my apartment, I asked him where he was staying. "I've moved into the guesthouse," he said, smiling, as though he had done something commendable!

At last!

"You've done what?!"

As I watched my new dream shatter into tiny pieces of irretrievable nothingness, I sat immobilized.

When, finally, he pulled up in front of my apartment, I jumped out of the car, and barked over my shoulder as I ran for my front door, "I never want to see you again!"

Once inside, I fell apart.

I was so angry I could hardly breathe.

I had been betrayed one more time.

Later that night, as I lay on my mattress on the floor in abject misery, the telephone rang. "I'm so sorry! Will you please forgive me? I really have moved out this time."

Twenty minutes later, my husband-to-be arrived at my front door with flowers. "We need to talk," he said anxiously.

It was now one o'clock in the morning. I wanted to slam the door in his face. But I also wanted him to hold me in his arms and tell me that he loved me.

Actually, I didn't know what I wanted.

He came in and I asked him to start a fire in the fireplace while I made some coffee. We talked throughout the remainder of the night.

The next morning, as the sun was rising, he kissed me tenderly and said, "Lady, I've been searching for you all of my life. Will you do me the honor of becoming my wife?"

"Yes, yes, yes!"

Oh my gosh! Everything was happening so fast.

Yes, Yes, Yes! Len left to shower and change. When he returned, we went out for a leisurely breakfast and then on to the office. Beaming, we strolled into the main hallway hand in hand.

Everyone stopped what they were doing. Because Len was so well liked by the men and women who worked with him, and because everybody seemed to know that he had been unhappily married for a long time, we were warmly received.

I immediately submitted my resignation.

Later that day, the new love of my life took me to Beverly Hills for a late lunch. After lunch, he said he wanted to introduce me to a good friend. The friend, it turned out, was a jeweler. I was shown two breath-taking diamonds, and both men encouraged me to select the one I liked best. After I had chosen, the jeweler told me that he would personally design a setting, for my stone.

All was right with the world.

Several days later, however, as we were driving home from an evening at the theater, my new fiancée' started talking about how much he was going to miss me while he was gone.

"Gone? Where are you going?" I asked.

"Jade, you know that I'm taking my parents to Europe," he carefully replied.

No! I did not know this.

"Honey, we've been planning this trip for more than a year. It will be my parents' last chance to go abroad. Besides, all four of us have had our shots."

All four of you have what? Then it began to dawn on me. "You're taking your wife on a trip to Europe?"

"I don't want to take her," he equivocated, "but my mother is counting on her support, because my mother is getting older."

I couldn't believe my ears. What in the world was he thinking? Was this explanation supposed to appeal to my sense of reasonableness?

Well, it did not.

"I can't cancel all of these reservations at this late date," he pleaded, "Please be reasonable. I've already booked all of the hotels, the tours and even a cruise."

It felt like a nuclear bomb had just been detonated inside of my head. My feelings of rage and disappointment were so intense that it took my breath away.

A nuclear explosion.

I could feel myself spiraling off into nowhere.

"You must keep it together" I told myself.

When his car finally pulled up in front of my apartment, I threw open the door and hissed in the most deadly tone I could muster, "If you go on that trip, I will not be here when you get back!"

I didn't wait for a reply. I stalked off.

Inside our apartment, I again fell apart, collapsing on my bed, I was too wounded to even cry.

Eventually, I did manage to drag myself into bed, and finally, I guess I must have drifted off to sleep.

The next morning, I felt as if I had been run over by a freight train. Staggering out into our dreadful little kitchen, I made myself a cup of very black coffee. I had a splitting headache.

Then the telephone rang... "I've canceled the trip. My mother is furious with me. I love you! Will you marry me?"

Safe at last.

Well, no, not quite yet.

Safe at last!

Several months before Len and I had connected, the company had sent formal invitations to several dozen scientists, inviting them to a weekend seminar in honor of the company's first three years in business.

This event was to culminate with a dinner at my now fiancé's former home. Unbeknownst to me, his soon to be ex-wife was still planning to host this affair, even though divorce proceedings had already begun.

My fiancé shared this information with me a week before the dinner (at his house) was to take place. He carefully explained that he and his soon to be ex-wife still mutually owned stock in the company and the upcoming weekend was very important.

Did he really think I would go along with this?

Listening to him drone on, and willing myself not to faint, I stared straight ahead.

When at last I felt some control, I said in a cold monotone, "this is not right, Len, it's just not right."

Darling...

"Darling...I can't cancel something this big at this late date."

I stared at him.

Finally he said, "Okay. Okay. I'll take care of it."

And he did!

One day before the distinguished guests were to arrive in Los Angeles, several secretaries spent the afternoon telephoning them to say there had been a change of plan: the Saturday night finale would now be held at a local hotel.

Len's company was composed of highly respected scientists, so you can imagine that none of these brilliant and privileged men were pleased with this latest development. However, when the night of the dinner party arrived, my fiancé was lovingly protective of me, and we sailed through the evening uneventfully.

We have now been married thirty-five years. And I still love him to the stars and back. He is my favorite person in the whole world. He is also a wonderful father figure to my children, who adore him.

He is our rock!

During the beginning days of our unusual and tempestuous courtship, I said "no" on three different occasions. Each time I said it, I feared it might mean the end of my dream.

Saying "no" to someone you are in love with is scary, since there can be disastrous consequences. But, I had been carefully taught that boundaries should be well defined *before* the wedding—not after. And, I trusted my mother because hadn't she had been right about shorthand and typing?

WHAT MEN HAVE TO SAY

When a mature man finds that he is attracted to a woman, his thinking goes something like this: "This woman is special. I could be happy with her and she will fit in with my friends, family and business associates. I want her!"

Being a disciplined adult, he probably does not share these thoughts with anyone.

When a grown man becomes aware that he is attracted to a woman, he thinks beyond his attraction and on to practical matters. Is she responsible? caring? fastidious? trustworthy?

> **Successful men operate in a different zone.**

Adult males tend to be skillful when assessing women. After a successful man has observed a woman, he can usually evaluate her pretty accurately.

But the successful man is often overly cautious. He studies a woman and then considers the long-term ramifications. The good news is that dynamic and well established adult males usually move quickly once they find the woman they have been looking for.

ALPHA MALES

Alpha males know there are more women in the world than men, so they can afford to be choosey.

When an alpha male is courting a woman, he expects to have nearly complete control. He is, after all, doing the inviting, the driving

> **High quality men decide almost immediately.**

and the paying. The more a woman allows an alpha male to take control, while he is courting her, the more irresistible she becomes to him. (Paradoxically, after marriage, alpha males do not want to stay in control; they then focus on their careers.)

The concept of control is relative. By allowing a man to be in control while he is courting you, you are actually shaping and controlling your own destiny. Achieving men usually let go of control once they have committed.

A man who is striving to get ahead wants a woman who will share the load and take some of the burden off his shoulders. This is fair: after all, he is the one responsible for carving out a space in the kingdom for you and the family. Power Players are the men who lead other men. They are responsible and tough minded, and have high standards for themselves and for others, so if

Become that special woman men dream of finding.

you are dreaming about marriage to a man of this caliber, you are dreaming of a man accustomed to being in charge. Such men want women who will support their endeavors.

Integrity is a must. Women with integrity know how to honor personal and business confidences. Honoring confidences is especially essential for men in positions of power.

I gave a simple questionnaire to several men I know personally. Some of the men I wanted to hear from are married, so I asked them to write about what they would look for in a woman if they were looking — or what they had been lucky enough to find. I assured each man that his response would be anonymous.

AN ENTERTAINMENT BIG WIG

In addition to being movie-star handsome, this first respondent is one of the nicest men I know.

"As I have a wife, married 25 years, my perspective might not be helpful, but I'll give it a shot. If I were looking for a wife, I would want a wife who:

❖ Would match and balance my temperament and interests

- ❖ Takes care of herself physically, emotionally, spiritually and mentally

- ❖ Cares about how she presents herself

- ❖ Is creative and is interested in creative endeavors and the arts

- ❖ Is open and interested in the world and in differences

- ❖ Would like to create a home with me

- ❖ Would be a partner and willing to share with me in the work and joy of creating a life

- ❖ A wife who would have her own outlets, friends and interests.

- ❖ A woman who would not be jealous of my having mine.

"My career has been in theatre and entertainment. I am blessed with a wife who has been willing to put up with eclectic friends, crazy projects, and long hours and strange places.

"As I read the points you stress in your book, my first reaction is that they seem, no offense, somewhat old-fashioned. As I think about it, however, the points you make are traits my wife seems to have employed with me. Some drive me nuts, some I have come to respect, some endear her to me."

A CHIEF EXECUTIVE OFFICER

"Desirable men operate in a different zone," this stand-up executive says, "and powerful men look for women who will make their lives easier." He went on to say that successful men realize that life is tough. They understand that women can be a liability as well as an asset. He concluded with, "A woman needs to be responsible enough with money to successfully manage my estate."

A PHYSICIAN

When this doctor walks into a room, his patients automatically know everything is going to be all right. This man is a natural healer.

"Thanks for your inquiry about the qualities possessed by my ideal woman. These are my thoughts:

- ❖ She needs to feel connected to God and have some form of spiritual life.

- ❖ She should love herself and others.

- ❖ I would hope she has done therapeutic work to better understand her own emotions.

- ❖ She needs to love me! She would inspire me to be the best man that I can be.

- ❖ She builds me up. She would value, honor and receive my love for her.

- ❖ She inspires me to reach for deeper levels of love, trust and joy."

A PSYCHOLOGIST

This man is polished, debonair, and sexually appealing.

"I believe in the common traits of maturity, courtesy, and humility. I like a woman who shares 50% of the time and is not afraid to talk about her likes and dislikes. I do like a woman who is appreciative, especially when I am picking up the tab.

"I go along with you on don't instruct or scold. I don't like to take direction or criticism from anybody. I have to admit, I love to be in charge.

"In your book you say, 'don't depend upon your mate for emotional security.' I agree wholeheartedly.

"I pay special attention to the following: personal hygiene, the way a woman keeps her home, the way she takes care of her children, the language she uses and the way she dresses.

"In your book you also say women should develop an interesting and complete life of their own. This might be the most important tenet of all, because it is the antidote to codependence. It's what I like the most about my wife.

"You talk about saving sex for last. I have dated a lot of women (yes he has!) and been married three times. For the first time, we saved sex for last. It's probably one of the reasons we are still together after 13 years."

A FOREIGN DIPLOMAT

Highly educated, sophisticated, socially accomplished and world traveled.

"Listening and not over talking are equally important to me. Instructing or scolding, either one, would instantly end the relationship.

Although I have been tempted, I have turned down relationships with younger women because I suspected they had issues with men.

Common interests are also very important to me."

A TWENTY-ONE YEAR OLD GARDENER

"What I am searching for in a woman now-a-days is hard to find. I need one that I can depend on emotionally – from a man's point of view. These are some of my points of view:

- ❖ A hard working woman.

- ❖ One that also has dreams and wants to make them a reality.

- ❖ One that falls and gets back up like nothing happened.

- ❖ One that knows how to cook and comes from a respectful family.

- ❖ I'm wishing she's not a flirt when I'm not looking.

- ❖ Sincere and open minded.

- ❖ Up for any challenge life might give us in the future.

- ❖ Clean and cheerful.

- ❖ And good in bed.

- ❖ Also to know her place in life.

- ❖ Doesn't spend more than what's intended financially.

- ❖ And if she has a hot body – perfect!"

AN ATTORNEY-AT-LAW

This attorney is always perfectly attired. He is bright, successful and devoted to his wife and family.

"I consider these the more important character traits of the perfect woman:

* ❖ Humorous, vivacious and willing to take a chance

* ❖ Minimally judgmental. Definitely spiritual

* ❖ Sociable and comfortable with herself

* ❖ Self-sufficient, intelligent and fun loving."

A JAZZ MUSICIAN

This man is empathetic, sensual and extremely sensitive.

"I want a woman with humor and intelligence, emotional stability, compatible values and shared interests and a woman who is physically attractive.

"Someone I can feel proud and confident of when introducing to my friends and family.

Some men have a lot to lose.

"I would be turned off by bad breath, crude language, too much talking or acting seductive. I would not want a competitor nor someone so self-involved that I would feel uncomfortable introducing her to others."

AN ASTROPHYSICIST

Considered a genius by his peers and one of the most powerful men I have ever known. He is a leader of men.

"Every woman should read this book," he says. "It addresses the principles of how best to intrigue and entice eligible men.

"In reality, it is a prescription for finding a way to a worthwhile life."

A LANDSCAPE ARCHITECT

This devoted family man is truly one of a kind.

"The way I thought before I got married is still the same way I think now. I think that women should have good qualities such as:

❖ She should respect herself and have good feelings.

❖ Be hard working and clean in her appearance and household.

❖ Take care of her man in marriage.

❖ Be a good mother to our children.

❖ Be faithful sexually and not cheat.

"For me these are good qualities."

SUCCESSFUL MEN ARE CAUTIOUS

Successful men want the admiration of other men, and they have very high standards when it comes to women. Therefore, they are usually cautious around available women.

Most desirable men past the age of 40 have lost interest in one-night-stands. They have done a lot of dating. They are bored! They have had numerous affairs. They are bored! Scores of women have chased them for years. They are bored! Successful men are looking for women with character who know how to listen.

Alpha males love to climb the highest mountains and ski the most challenging slopes. These super-powered fellows are not intrigued by women who are clingy. They want women who are independent. They can't abide women who try to take charge.

She sounded great on the phone.

Dynamic men have their share of anxieties. Underneath their impressive self-confidence, they may be concerned about losing what they have acquired. They may secretly wonder if they are good enough. They may fear they don't deserve the success they have achieved. They may wonder if they are clever enough and tough enough to hold on to it.

When it comes to permanent commitment, these men are very cautious. Since they have spent years working hard and competing, they have learned to keep their own counsel. They are often skittish when it comes to intimacy. They usually fear emotional intimacy.

Life with one of these high octane fellows will be more demanding and challenging than life with a more easy-going man. Self-assured men do a lot of testing. Less successful men are likely to be more accepting.

AN EXCLUSIVE DATING SERVICE

"I am the divorced father of an eleven year old son. I am successful and financially secure, and I have learned through the hard school of internet dating that truth in advertising does not always apply.

When you're a busy guy looking for a woman with whom to share your life, a dating service can seem appealing.

After joining one of the more exclusive services, strange women I had only talked with on the phone or emailed were falling all over me.

I finally agreed to meet one of them. We fell into bed almost instantly.

Okay! I didn't fight her off, but I soon wished I had.

The next woman, whose good looks attracted me, seemed delightful over the phone and on line, so I invited her to have lunch with me. Why do women post 12 year old pictures on the net? Why do women say they love hiking when they can't climb up a steep hill?

Fear of emotional intimacy.

I was more than a little startled at the difference between this woman's up-close-and-personal and her picture. But I soldiered on.

Lunch became one long confessional. By the end of it, I learned much more about her than I wanted to know.

At the end of lunch, she invited me to her place for a second cup of coffee, but I told her I had a business meeting, and I split.

I said I would keep in touch. But I never contacted her again."

TOO MUCH INTIMACY

"It took a year after my wife's death before I started thinking about dating again.

I quickly learned it's a scary new world out there, even for a fairly self confident guy.

After one date, women seem to feel that e-mails several times a day will endear them.

Trust me, they don't.

When I got calls on my cell phone before I have even called to suggest a second date, I run for cover.

I am a successful man in my early fifties. I run a successful company and I am used to working with strong women. But, when women start looking for commitment after one date, I run for the hills.

I don't expect women to be silent, but neither do I want to hear a woman's life's story on the first date.

For me, this is too much intimacy. To protect myself, I no longer give out my e-mail address or my cell phone number.

My date from hell was a casual acquaintance that I asked to have dinner with me. Dinner was fine, but upon returning to her condo, she invited me in, saying she wanted to lend me a book.

Suddenly this woman started talking about how totally she was going to please me sexually. She would fulfill my every fantasy.

All I could think of was 'How the f--- am I going to escape?'

After this experience, I have become ever more wary of women who see me as their answer."

WHAT MAKES SUCCESSFUL MEN TICK?

My husband and I have a friend who has been divorced for several years. While I do not always agree with this bachelor's philosophical take on women, I feel his perceptions are representative.

I think you can learn a lot about how dynamic men think by taking a peek into this good-looking bachelor's mind.

Jack (not his real name) has two grown children. He is six-foot-two, unusually good-looking, athletic and professionally successful. He has always been good with women. In fact, women can't seem to resist him.

I asked Jack if I could ask him some questions and use his answers for this book.

"Of course!" he said, laughing.

Women are forever inviting Jack to do things. I suspect most of them sleep with him on the first date, although Jack does not say so.

He did tell me that he has never had to "go after" a woman, adding with a grin that he has never found it necessary. He volunteered that he just stands around, until some woman finds him! The women who find Jack are very beautiful.

Our good-looking friend admitted that he didn't think he has ever been in love. He added that he knows he has missed out on something important.

Jack was dating yet another woman, and asked if we would like to meet her. (He usually invites my husband and me to join him when an exciting new woman comes into his life.)

We see a lot of Jack.

"She's charming, witty and well-connected, but she is subtly inching her way into my life. I want to know what you think of her before this goes any further," he said.

"If you think she's so terrific, Jack, why are you so hesitant?" I asked him.

"Because some of the time she makes me feel like a hunted animal! However, other times, she can be soft and nurturing, so I'm confused."

Jack suddenly changed the subject. "Skiing," he said, "is similar to pursuing a woman, both take a great deal of effort." I assumed that Jack was finished when then he added:

"There is so much you have to go through for a few minutes of ecstasy!"

I think our gorgeous friend was saying that, this time, he wasn't sure the ecstasy was worth the effort.

"She's a terrific lady," he continued, as though trying to convince himself, "but, she sticks to me like glue. She can think of more reasons to come over to my place. I don't like that clingy thing. I want to live my life while she lives hers. I don't want someone who's waiting around for me and doesn't have a life until I enter the picture."

I asked our handsome bachelor friend if he thought he would ever get married again.

"I would like to marry again, sure. But I am equally content to remain a bachelor. However, I do understand that the best way to live is with a woman with whom you are truly compatible. But, just being with a woman is low on my list of priorities."

He is seldom without a beautiful woman on his arm.

Jack admitted that he knew he had made a mistake or two in his life. "Having a trophy wife is no longer a priority for me," he went on, "and I've learned a thing or two from my mistakes. I don't plan on making those same mistakes again.

When women start clutching, I run! Well…I don't necessarily stop seeing them. Actually, I just create distance and put them in a casual category."

Putting women in a casual category means Jack still enjoys having sex with them, but they no longer hold a significant place in his life. (I felt a little numb after hearing Jack talk so candidly.)

Moving forward…I asked Jack what he would be looking for, if he were looking for a wife.

"I would be looking for a woman with the following characteristics," he said.

- ❖ Someone not more than ten years my junior.

- ❖ Someone very fit.

- ❖ Someone attractive, not necessarily beautiful, but fit and trim.

- ❖ Someone with her own interests: I don't want to be her answer.

- ❖ Someone who likes sports: skiing, hiking, tennis.

- ❖ Someone with a good education, formal or informal.

- ❖ Someone with high energy and a sense of humor.

"I want to be able to talk politics, economics, business and sports with any woman who is seriously in my life. I'm no longer a testosterone terrorist. If I were to make a commitment at this age, I would be looking for a woman who has real value.

"I would be looking for someone who would:

- ❖ Not sulk for days on end.

- ❖ Not go berserk and then take it out on me.

- ❖ Not complain constantly.

❖ Not feel the need to compete with me.

❖ Not flirt with other men.

❖ Not try to take charge.

❖ Not give me gifts all the time.

❖ Not make constant demands on my time.

"I would be seriously attracted to a woman who...

❖ Doesn't chase after me.

❖ Goes into intimacy slowly.

❖ Doesn't criticize.

❖ Has some spiritual commitment.

❖ Likes to listen.

❖ Has a positive, upbeat attitude.

❖ Is sophisticated, but also thoughtful and kind.

❖ Does not have a long list of past sexual partners."

"I would want a woman who is soft and gentle. I spend my days with aggressive and sometimes disagreeable people. When I come home at night, I would want to spend time with someone who was a good friend.

"Empathy is important. I have to be steady and levelheaded all day long. When I come home at night, I would want to have someone waiting for me who cares about my struggles. I'm not looking for additional challenges.

"An easy-going nature is important. I would be looking for a woman who is at peace with herself. I don't want to live with someone who is intent on defending the rights of womankind.

"Fitness is important too. I would want a wife I could be proud of. However, beauty is definitely not my number one priority.

"Given the superficiality of life today, a capacity for emotional intimacy is very important to me. How delightful it would be to find a woman who is capable of emotional intimacy, someone unguarded who doesn't consider men the enemy. It wouldn't take long for a woman like this to get all of my attention."

Successful men are usually well informed. They often belong to health clubs and take good care of their bodies. They are usually involved in community activities. They may have meaningful religious affiliations. If you are looking for a man like this, you have set your sights near the top of the ladder.

These men are a special breed. They are hard-hitting and accustomed to winning. They demand excellence from themselves and those around them. Because they are often targets of opportunists, they have learned not to trust. You will have to demonstrate your trustworthiness in order to earn their respect.

Successful men usually approach business, sports and women in the same manner. Life experiences may have taught them that women are more interested in their money than in them.

A TAD TOO SELF-INVOLVED?

When dating dynamic men, you may find they do not always have a driving need to please you. Women have, for too long, been working hard to please them. Women have called them on the phone, been available at the last minute, cooked intimate little dinners and eagerly agreed to sex.

While waiting to find their ideal woman, these men may enjoy casual sex, but when a super-achiever thinks in terms of marriage, his woman must be someone special! The man who is in a position to choose is probably looking for a woman with the positive attributes of his mother, minus his mother's negative qualities.

> **Dynamic men should be approached with due caution.**

Since top-notch men are attracted to women who know their own value, it is incumbent upon *you*, when you are dating one of these fine fellows, to take very good care of yourself.

One of the more obvious drawbacks of marriage to a powerfully driven man is that he is not always capable of being warm and nurturing. Nor will he always be available. When you need someone to comfort you, he may fall short. He probably intends to be loving, but he may not be able to make you feel better about what hurts. The scale of problems he is dealing with in his professional life may make your concerns seem somewhat less than monumental.

The high-testosterone man is not a good mommy. You will need to turn to your mother when you have a fight with your boss, or the couch you ordered shows up in the wrong color.

Dynamic men tend to be self-centered. During the course of an evening, for instance, they may not ask one question about you! But be patient. If you give them time, they will eventually respond positively. When powerful guys fall, they will want to know everything there is to know about you.

Powerful men — educated or not-so-educated — are usually fiercely loyal and protective of their women. Once they make up their minds that a woman is worthy, they can become very devoted. But forget about outwitting these men. The self-assured man may give his power to you, but he will not let you take it.

HE WAS A FOUR STAR GENERAL

Strong men fall into two categories: those striving to get ahead and those who have already arrived. The following story describes how a self-confident man can make a woman feel desirable, while a more insecure man may cause her to doubt herself.

My husband and I had been married only a short time when Len asked me if I would host a cocktail party at our home.

"There will be forty scientists, plus several military officers and a four-star general," he said. "You and the wife of the president will be the only women attending."

I asked my new husband why there would be no other women, and he mumbled something about the cocktail party being work related.

I was newly married and not that sure of myself, so the thought of hosting a party for forty scientists and a four-star general scared me half-to-death.

During the following week, I thought about little else. What should I wear? What kind of hors d'oeuvres should I serve? Will I be self-confident enough to appear gracious?

On the day of the cocktail party I was, more-or-less, relaxed because I felt I had covered all of the bases. As our house began filling up with serious-looking men in dark suits, I wasn't so sure. And, the general had not arrived.

I cornered Len in the kitchen and asked what had happened to the general.

"He's here. He's just not in uniform," my husband said, not paying much attention to me.

Before I could question him further, our doorbell rang and he hurried off. No matter! I could certainly recognize a four-star general when I saw one, and sure enough, within seconds, I spotted him.

He was tall, fit and immaculately dressed. He was wearing a black Armani suit with a crisply starched white shirt and a red paisley Brioni tie. Very intimidating!

Nevertheless, I walked right over and introduced myself. I began asking him appropriate questions. I listened carefully to his responses, keeping my eyes focused on him. But, somehow I found myself having trouble staying focused on him.

"Shame," I scolded myself. I tried to listen more earnestly. But my mind kept wandering off to other things. I simply could not stay focused on this important man.

I finally excused myself and began mingling with our other guests. I couldn't find a safe place to light, and then I spotted four men standing off in a corner of the dining room who looked much less austere than the others. I purposefully walked over to them.

Testing her assumptions.

When I got close enough to speak, three of the four men moved away, leaving only a rather ordinary-looking man in a rumpled tweed jacket. Although this man was powerfully built, he had a relaxed easiness about him which made him seem safe.

I breathed a sigh of relief!

"May I stand next to you for a few minutes," I asked. "I need to get my bearings: I have been trying to engage our guest of honor in conversation, and I just made a mess of it."

> **Things may not be as obvious as they seem.**

Smiling broadly, the relaxed and comfortable-looking gentleman said, "My dear, please allow me to introduce myself. I'm General Burt Spivey."

I thought I was going to faint!

I could barely stammer some inane reply. Within minutes, however, this eminently distinguished man had put me completely at ease.

Lucky me! I had General Spivey pretty much to myself for most of the remainder of the cocktail party. I found him absolutely fascinating.

Later that night, as my husband and I were cleaning up after our party, I complained about the abrasive man in the Armani suit; the one I had thought to be General Spivey. I ranted on and on about how rude that man had been.

Clearly amused, my husband told me that the man whom I had found so unpleasant was only the administrator of an obscure agency, and he had just that day been asked to take early retirement. (He had been fired!)

I have found that men who have successfully proven themselves in the world are almost always well disciplined, highly intelligent and accepting of others. They are accepting of other, that is, until they are challenged. When that happens... watch out!

BECOMING A MAN MAGNET

The most respected minds in history seem to agree that everything we do in private comes back to us: to either haunt us or glorify us. The mistake women make is thinking they can do a little of this and a little of that and no one will be the wiser.

Not true! Have you ever heard of a woman who was half-pregnant? We are either honest or dishonest, moral or immoral, big-hearted or self-seeking. Any woman who thinks she can be both is fooling only herself. Indecisive, wishy-washy women who can't make up their minds always lose.

A tiny infraction may disqualify you.

We are either women of value or we are not women of value. The secret to success is admitting to ourselves which kind of women we are. I have worked with scores of women who have found the man of their dreams by simply becoming more self-focused.

A women hoping to marry well must address herself to first cleaning up her own act, because she needs to be perceived as an asset. The tiniest infraction (unwashed hair, chipped fingernails, or unpolished shoes) can disqualify her from consideration by a man who has choices.

Dating is competitive and much like a job interview. When you submit your resume, you will be evaluated against dozens of other applicants. If your resume has staggered margins, misspelled words or poor spacing, these seemingly minor errors can take you out of the race…even though you may have exceptional qualifications. Lack of attention to detail will be noticed, and may disqualify you.

Think about the qualities you are hoping to find in the right man. Doesn't he have to be a person you can trust? Someone the world looks up to? Fit? Sexually appealing? His life in good order? Well, guess what? Men have the same requirements.

KEEP YOUR EYE ON THE PRIZE

In order to end up with a man of value, you must be steadfast; you will want to make up your mind and not compromise.

As I have already stated, successful men have demanding standards, and they can also be harsh judges. They judge women not

---

only by their physical appearance, but also by their behavior and moral code.

A MIRROR REFLECTION

The man you long to connect with will be a mirror reflection of you. But that isn't quite accurate, more accurately, the men who pursue you will have the same number of points that you have.

If you are an 85% successful woman, he will be an 85% successful man, even though his 85% may be in entirely different areas.

You may be a hard hitting professional. He may be skilled at dealing with people.

You may be a compulsive shopper. He may be cavalier about paying his bills. You may be fiercely loyal. He may make friends easily.

You may be resolutely disciplined. He may be capable of multi-tasking.

But... your sum totals will be identical! You will each be 85% successful. If you doubt what I am saying, look around you at the couples you know.

ACTION IS THE MAGIC WORD

Direct action is always more effective than threats and cajoling. Ranting, raving and threatening only weakens you. Don't tell him. Show him.

Now consider the following. My husband and I had been married only a few weeks when we were invited to a company party honoring my new husband. Shortly after arriving at the party, a group of scientists surrounded my husband and a very seductive blonde began flirting with him!

He entertained everyone by being his most droll and entertaining self. The more-than-well-built blonde seemed captivated. Watching this from the sidelines, where I had been saddled with someone's irritating wife, I began a slow boil.

When I concluded that I could no longer endure watching, I walked over to my husband, asked him for the car keys and left the party.

I drove home.

My husband finally realized that I was no longer at the gala given in his honor, and was livid with anger. He immediately called a cab. When I heard our front door open and then bang shut, I knew he was furious.

**Taking action —
when it is called for.**

He bounded up the stairs two at a time. The minute he reached our bedroom doorway, he began bellowing.

"How dare you humiliate me in front of my colleagues!" he raged.

"How dare you flirt with that cheap blonde!" I screamed back.

From there, we escalated into a near nuclear explosion which scared us both. Calming down, we finally surrendered to a long and carefully controlled discussion. We came to an agreement: In the future, he would not flirt with other women. I would never leave a social event without first letting him know.

Although what I did that day is outrageous by societal standards, I think this anecdote illustrates the point that actions by themselves can be very powerful and effective.

IS THAT OK SHE ASKS

She was an accomplished professional, as well as the mother of four children. She had a successful husband who was devoted to her.

Women were constantly seeking this woman's counsel, because she obviously understood how to live successfully with a powerful man. She also knew how to take care of herself.

"I have always been the boss in our family, even though my husband is a powerful leader.

He began allowing me to take charge of our family's affairs after only a few years of marriage. My secret is the way I speak to him.

"I always end my sentences with, 'Is that ok with you?' I'm not really asking. It is just something I learned to say that works. "For example:

"We need to take a vacation. 'Is that OK with you?'

"Let's go out for dinner tonight. 'OK?'

"I'm going shopping for some new outfits tomorrow. 'OK with you?'

"My husband is a rather controlling, macho guy and likes to be in control. Yet, I have controlled ninety-five percent of our social life and our money for years. But...I never forget to end my sentences with 'OK'.

"If I were to decide to take over without including 'OK?' it would never work. He would **Is that OK?** stop me in a New York minute. But, as long as I end my sentences with: 'Is that OK?' he seems to be totally accepting."

THROWING CAUTION TO THE WIND

T he Right Person! The Right Time! The Right Place! And the best intentions fly out the window!

When you are dating a man you are sexually attracted to, it is not always easy to make the right decision. Therefore, seeing some mistakes in judgment other women have made may prove helpful.

SHE KNEW THE TRUTH – BUT SHE IGNORED IT

Although he told me we would be spending the whole weekend together, he didn't arrive until late Saturday afternoon. The next morning, after a night of fabulous sex, I suggested we go riding together, because I own two magnificent horses. He told me that he couldn't stay, because he had things to do in town.

He dressed quickly, gave me a peck on the cheek, and left.

He didn't call me all week, so I finally called him. I told him we needed to talk. He suggested I come into town and have dinner with him. Having dinner with him meant that I cooked. Something inside of me knew that this wasn't quite right, but I went anyway. I really wanted to see him.

I fixed a lovely dinner for us, which we enjoyed by candlelight. It had been my intention to have a serious talk after dinner, but we ended up making love instead. Then it was too late to talk. I drove myself home, and I haven't heard from him since.

You invited a man to spend the weekend with you and He did not arrive on time? You should have sent him packing. His actions told you that he considered you a good sex partner, rather than a potential life partner.

SHE FORGOT SHE WAS HIS GUEST

My boyfriend asked me if I would like to fill in at a men's tennis game at his club. I said I would love to. We had a great game, and afterward they asked me to join them for lunch.

During lunch, I took an active part in the conversation and thoroughly enjoyed myself.

But, ever since that day, my boyfriend has cooled down.

When a woman is asked to join a group of men for lunch, the men are hoping she will mostly listen. You forgot that this was a man's luncheon group and you were only a guest.

HE CAME ON SO STRONG

We had been dating steadily, and then suddenly, without warning, he told me he wasn't going to be seeing me anymore.

But now he has started calling again, and I see him once a week. But I never see him on weekends.

When a man isn't seeing you on weekends, it probably means he is seeing someone else.

SHE MAY HAVE EMBARRASSED HIM

I was in love, so for his birthday, I invited his best friend, and his friend's wife, to join us for dinner at my club.

The four of us got along very well. After dinner, as we were waiting for an elevator to take us to the club's subterranean garage, the two men became engrossed in conversation.

When the elevator arrived, we all stepped inside, but neither man made any move to press the down button. So...I reached across my date's chest and pressed the button myself.

As the elevator began descending, he gave me the most disapproving look.

When you reached across your friend's chest and pressed the down button, you probably embarrassed him. After all, he was probably already a bit uncomfortable being your guest.

HE SMILED AND THEN SAID, "CALL ME"

I was having lunch with a girlfriend when a man I knew stopped at our table and started talking to me. He chatted for a few minutes, and then as he was leaving, handed me his card, and asked me to call him sometime.

How rude! He should have asked for your phone number.

SHE SENT HIM A THANK YOU NOTE

I was attending a boring party when someone introduced me to a very good looking man. After talking for a few minutes, he asked if I wanted to duck out and catch a movie.

I said I would love to.

He started calling or seeing me every day. Several weeks later, he invited me to have dinner with him, saying he would cook for me.

I drove to his house. We had dinner together and then he made love to me.

The next morning, I sent him a little note thanking him for a lovely evening. But now he has stopped calling.

Men are not intrigued by such availability. The harder a man has to work, the more desirable a woman becomes.

SHE WANTED TO WIN HIM OVER BUT...

A man that I knew invited me to have lunch with him. During lunch, our conversation turned to his recent divorce.

He told me he was concerned about his ex-wife. He couldn't make up his mind whether to send her flowers or perhaps a note expressing his sorrow over the breakup of their marriage. Or… maybe a quiet dinner for two would be nice.

What did I think?

I explained that he was no longer responsible for his ex-wife. He should be concentrating on his own life. I haven't heard from him since.

Men may seek a woman's advice, but they usually don't appreciate her for giving it. This is a lose-lose situation. Better to have sympathized with him and assured him that he would work it out himself.

THE BIRTHDAY PARTY THAT BACKFIRED

I gave my boyfriend a surprise birthday party. I thought he would be thrilled. But he was sullen and petulant during his party and later seemed almost indifferent when we made love.

Most men do not appreciate this kind of attention from women they are only dating. It smacks of entrapment.

HE WAS TALL, DARK AND HANDSOME

While vacationing in Hawaii, friends asked if I would like to have dinner with a man coming over from the mainland. They said he was good-looking and very rich. I said, definitely.

Their friend called me from California and we talked for over an hour. Before hanging up, he asked if I would join him for dinner the night he arrived.

That night, when I opened my door and first saw him, I was stunned: he was positively gorgeous. He took me to the Ritz-Carlton, and throughout dinner kept telling me how beautiful I was.

Before taking me back to my condo, he asked if I would spend the night with him. I demurred. At my door, he kissed me tenderly and said he would call me when he got back to the mainland. He has never called.

Sometimes a woman doesn't get to know why.

BEEN THERE — DONE THAT

A good friend of mine has uncommon wisdom. But, over the years, I found myself moving further and further away from her, because it was so painful watching the disrespectful way her husband treated her.

Six months ago, we accidentally ran into each other and decided to have lunch and catch up. She seemed different. She was stronger yet softer, and she was more centered. I asked her how things were going.

"I thought several times about leaving my husband," she said, "but unfortunately I love him. So I took a workshop on love addictions. As I started applying the things I learned, I was dumbfounded by the results. My friend said she was anxious to share what she had learned with other women, so I jotted down in shorthand what she was saying as she was saying it. These are the points she made:

- ❖ Too much dependence on another person kills romance, and it may eventually kill you.

- ❖ Every time he neglects you, and you take it, you lose a piece of you. That small part of you does not come back. Eventually there is no one left inside of you to even call out for help.

- ❖ The man in your life tells you that "if" you hadn't acted so badly, he wouldn't have had to react the way he did. So you try to do better…because you think your life depends on his loving you. But, no matter how hard you try, things don't get better. And all the while, he gets stronger. Eventually he may leave you because he finds someone more exciting.

- ❖ Those three magic words: I love you, I need you, and I want you. Those sugar-coated words can sometimes become a prison cell.

- ❖ Abusive men need to control. They expect you to jump when they whistle. As long as you keep jumping, they will keep on dishing it out.

- ❖ 'Less-than' men can be very hurtful. Usually these men are not successful in the work arena, so they take out their frustration on you. Don't let them!

- ❖ Don't be a punching bag.

- ❖ Reacting is an impulse. It is not a measured decision.

- ❖ Whenever there is a nice period, you think everything is fixed. Then suddenly "boom" and everything is bad again. And you are back where you started from.

- ❖ Women always think it is their fault, but that is not necessarily true. Most women are too willing to sell themselves down the river.

- ❖ Try and see him as he really is — not as you want him to be.

- ❖ Don't work to make things happen. Wait for things to happen.

- ❖ We can't change them, because we are powerless over other people

- ❖ You must not allow men to treat you badly.

Clear boundaries are essential.

- ❖ Do not get into angry discussions. In the long run, it is better to withdraw.

- ❖ If you can't accept him as he is, move on.

- ❖ Some men are harsh and snappy most of the time. Women tell themselves, "But, he doesn't mean it." Oh yes he does!

- ❖ Some people live in the light. But, some people live in darkness.

- ❖ Clear boundaries are essential.

- ❖ If he doesn't pick up the phone and call you, he doesn't want to talk to you.

- ❖ Positive thinking people (men) reinforce us. Negative people (men) suck us dry.

- ❖ Don't try to force solutions.

- ❖ We say to ourselves, "There must be something else I can do." Wrong!

- ❖ He can be hateful and indifferent — then suddenly switch and be strong and caring. You are baffled. "What did I do wrong? What did I say that I shouldn't have?" Probably nothing!

- ❖ Be slow in making decisions. Quick decisions usually backfire.

- ❖ If you pray, why worry. If you worry, why pray? ⟵

ESTABLISHING APPROPRIATE BOUNDARIES

Boundaries keep a woman safe. But some women see only what they want to see and this is called denial. And once patterns have been set it is more difficult to establish boundaries.

Having clearly defined boundaries give you power. Clear boundaries also make you more desirable.

I insist that my dates arrive on time.

I expect them to phone if they are going to be late. If they don't call, I won't be at home when they finally arrive.

I demand respect because I respect myself.

If he flirts with another woman, I'll call a cab and leave. I must demonstrate self-respect before I can command respect from a man.

I expect the same consideration he gives his boss. *business associates.*

Why should I put up with less?

I never accept last-minute invitations. *?*

I have no intention of being a last minute thought. "I'm sorry, I have other plans."

I do not engage in casual sex

I am a woman of value, not a one-night-stand. I want to be treated like I am someone special.

THE NO SANDWICH

Saying "no" to a man, and sticking to your guns, requires self-discipline. But it is easier to say "no" once you know how. I learned how to do this from a Beverly Hills psychologist a long time ago. This is what she suggested:

- ❖ Give the person (man) a wonderful positive.

    "I like you so much."

- ❖ Give him another positive.

    "I have such fun when I'm with you.

- ❖ Slip in your "no."

    "But I'm not comfortable having sex so soon."

- ❖ Finish with another strong positive.

    "I really like you, I'm just not ready."

Your "no" is much less offensive when it is slipped in between two strong positives. You may find this helpful in other areas of your life as well.

HAVE YOU EVER EATEN DUMPSTER STEW?

This is an unbelievable tale about a bona-fide heiress who comes from a prominent New York family. She is brilliant, hilariously funny and liked by both men and women.

Elizabeth was in her early forties at the time of this story, and with the help of just a touch of plastic surgery, she was still hypnotically beautiful.

She had been divorced for several years, but she and her children were still living in their large beachfront home in Malibu. Both her home and her car were always in serious disarray, although she herself was always immaculately groomed.

Did I mention that she was a medical doctor with a thriving practice?

Now, wouldn't you think that a woman of this caliber would be smart enough to stay away from a struggling UCLA graduate student? Elizabeth became involved with just such a man: He was fifteen years her junior.

Jonathan drove a beat-up Volkswagen van and was living hand-to-mouth. He was tall, good-looking and charming. Most women found him fascinating, including me.

One day, as Elizabeth and I were having coffee at Starbucks, she told me she was living with Jonathan part time. She said she had decided to test their relationship by adopting Jonathan's lifestyle. (This is a true story!)

Elizabeth smiled and added, "I'll bet you didn't know that Jonathan's home has an ocean view."

No, I did not know this.

"He has built himself a home by tunneling into the side of the bluffs overlooking the ocean, and his place has all of the accouterments. It has a stove, a queen-size mattress, bedding, rugs, lanterns and cooking utensils."

Elizabeth continued, "Jonathan has furnished his place with the things he finds on curbs on garbage-collection days. People in our town throw away very nice things. His cave house is surprisingly comfortable: he even has running water."

It seems that Jonathan had taken a long garden hose and tapped into the water spigot of one of the houses on the bluff above his cave home.

With a sly grin, Elizabeth continued. "I have been spending several nights a week with him."

I was stupefied!

She gleefully went on, "Have you ever eaten dumpster stew, Jade?"

"Dumpster stew?"

"Its stew," she explained, "made from discarded meat bones and day old vegetables."

Elizabeth explained that she and Jonathan would sneak out late at night, scavenge vegetables from the dumpsters at Gelson's (an upscale market in the neighborhood) and make stew.

This debutante? This medical doctor?

"The stew is delicious," she airily continued. "You and Len will have to join us for dinner some night soon."

Remember, I knew her well, and I knew she was serious. But I could also see by the laugh lines around her eyes that she was thoroughly enjoying herself, at my expense.

In truth, I thought it might be fun to see how she and Jonathan were living. But I knew my serious scientist husband would never agree to dinner in a cave.

After our coffee session, I did not see Elizabeth again for months. When next we met, she tearfully told me that Jonathan had broken off their affair. She looked like death itself, and said she said she was having a terrible time getting over what she persisted in calling "my little fling."

Although Elizabeth is an accredited physician, and continued to manage the pressures of her medical practice successfully, she was falling apart emotionally. As a result of what she continued to refer to as her "nothing relationship," she was suffering untold emotional distress. She told me she was humiliated, and also furious with herself, for having been so foolish.

A year later, Elizabeth and I met for lunch and she brought me up to date. She had quit drinking, she said, and was seeing a psychiatrist twice a week. She now had employed a full-time housekeeper as well as an efficient personal assistant.

She looked radiant. "I've gone back to church, and I'm playing tennis twice a week," she said.

Are you wondering what happened next?

Of course she met a man! Her husband is a significant personage, and they have now been married for ten years.

In Elizabeth's desire for emotional escape and sexual gratification, she almost lost her chance for a decent life. But, unlike other women, this medical doctor knuckled-down and corrected the mistakes she had been making.

Elizabeth and I aren't close any more, although I do see her occasionally. She still practices medicine and, as always, is drop-dead gorgeous. She is still very much married.

I hope this true story will be a source of encouragement for you if you are struggling to overcome a similar mistake in judgment.

THE DATING GAME

enerally speaking, first dates are the most important. This is the time to set boundaries. The boundaries you set (or don't set) become the guidelines for the rest of the relationship.

Women need to stay on full alert.

With this thought in mind, I urge you to decide ahead of time how you want to be treated. Remember, the man you are dating will never again be as anxious to please you.

After a first date, you are in a unique position to look into your own future. If you chose to be insightful, you can take a good look at the man's life: his job, his family interactions, his children (if he has any) his financial status, where he lives, the car he drives, his clothes, his physique, his hobbies and his general attitude about life.

If you look closely and are honest with yourself, you will discover exactly what to expect should you decide to spend the rest of your life with him. This process is called using your head before you allow your heart to get involved.

Approach dating at least as seriously as job hunting.

Again, the important thing to remember is that the man you are dating will never again be as willing to please you. Unfortunately, the average woman does not seem to understand this concept. But really smart women do!

Sophisticated women know the significance of first encounters. Consequently, they approach all-important dates the same way they approach an important job interview. Seriously!

When being interviewed, smart women know they should listen attentively, ask intelligent questions, stay focused, and refrain from talking too much about themselves. In other words, in-the-know women know how to make a good first impression.

Now, desirable men are always pursued by eager women. But, most of those women will be making mistakes that I hope you will not be making. Remember: the woman who makes the fewest mistakes wins.

Mistakes made by the average woman include: agreeing to meet men half-way, paying part of the tab, cooking intimate dinners for two, running errands for (or with) men, and saying "yes" to sex before they have a serious commitment.

You will stand out from other women, if you do not do these things. And the less accommodating you are the more successful you will be with high caliber men.

WOMEN NEED TO USE THEIR HEADS

Since focus is an imperative for the woman hoping to marry well, I am amazed at the number of women who put their brains into cold storage when they date. I think there is truth in the old saying, "If you don't know where you're going, you're not likely to get there.

> **What would life be like married to this man?**

Yes. Women need to use their heads. And one way to do this is to figure out ahead of time what you want. I suggest writing a list of requirements and tucking it away for future reference.

MORE ABOUT FIRST DATES

At the end of a first date, you should ask yourself how you feel: Do I feel beautiful? Do I feel desirable? Do I feel vibrant and alive? Or...Do I feel I should lose some weight? Should I be working out more? Would collagen help? What about a partial face-lift?

Only those men who feel good about themselves can make you feel good about you. Unless you feel radiant and alive after you have been out with a man, you should not go out with him again!

After you have dated a man a few times, ask yourself some more questions:

❖ If I were to marry this man and I had the flu: Will he bring me chicken soup? Will he drive me to the doctor? Or...will he need to keep his scheduled golf game?

❖ If my parents were in need, will he be there for them? Or...will he be too busy at his office?

❖ If I have children from a previous marriage, will he act as a father figure? Or will he cordially ignore them?

❖ If I gain weight, will he still have eyes for only me? Or...will he begin to ogle other women?

❖ If I refuse him sexually, will he accept my "not tonight" graciously? Or...will he pout and punish?

If, additionally, you want to find out how he will treat you once you are married to him, pay attention to how he relates to his mother.

If your guesses about the man you have been dating are more negative than positive, you need to think about calling a halt, while you still can. Remember, it is easier to stop something unpleasant *before* it gets started, than it is to stop it once it is going full speed.

MEN MAKE INSTANT JUDGMENTS

Since men respond to the way we present ourselves, it is up to us to take responsibility for the impressions we make.

For instance, men make instant judgments about the role a woman will play in their lives, whether a potential life-partner, casual sex partner, possible good friend or only an acquaintance. These instant male judgments are based upon the way women have presented themselves.

Since all men make these instantaneous gut-level evaluations, presentation is all important. Because...once a man has made up his mind, he is usually slow to change it.

A FIFTY FOOT YACHT

During the time that I was single, I worked as a part-time paralegal in a prestigious Beverly Hills Law Firm. I was young, attractive and yearning for excitement.

I was also stupid.

After working for less than a week, the office manager, whom I barely knew, asked if I would like to go sailing with one of the firm's partners. She told me that she had dated this man herself, and was sure I would like him.

The partner she was touting was somewhat older than I, but I still found him very attractive. And, he was rich. Although we had never been properly introduced, I had heard that he was newly divorced.

She knew she was going to be raped.

I said I would love to go sailing.

Late the next afternoon, the senior partner called and asked if I would like to go sailing with him the next day. Totally disregarding all that I had been taught about last minute invitations, I said yes.

Early the next morning, my debonair blind date arrived right on time, driving a new, top-of-the-line Mercedes coupe. The man himself was as impressive as his car: he was very tall, well built, physically fit and totally self-assured.

During our drive to the Marina, he couldn't have been more charming, and when we arrived at his slip, I found his fifty-two-foot sailboat as impressive as the man himself. Since I love to sail and had not been sailing for years, I was brimming over with excitement.

Once underway, my exciting date went below and a few minutes later came topside with crystal wine glasses, a bottle of expensive wine and a wicker basket filled with gourmet sandwiches.

The sun was shining and there wasn't a cloud in the sky. I was soon lulled into a state of hypnotic bliss and contentment. As the winds whipped our sails and the sea lapped at the sides of the boat, I slipped into a euphoric fantasy about sharing my life with this fabulous Beverly Hills attorney.

A heavenly day.

My blind date was a seasoned skipper, and I was very impressed with his easy command of his yacht. His extraordinary good looks only added fuel to a fire that was already blazing away inside my head.

Needless risk.

At the end of our day on the high seas, as we were docking the sailboat, he asked if I was free to join him for dinner.

Of course I was free!

My debonair escort took me to an elegant oceanfront restaurant that featured slow music and soft candlelight. During dinner, he continued to fascinate me with his polish and sophistication.

On the drive back to my house, I asked if he would like to stop for a cup of coffee before getting back on the freeway. He said that he would love a second cup of coffee.

The minute I finished inviting him for coffee, I remembered having said earlier that my children were spending the weekend with their father. But, there was no reason to be concerned with a man of this caliber. He was, after all, a full partner in one of the most prestigious law firms in Beverly Hills.

When we arrived at our house, I turned on background music and asked him to make himself comfortable, while I went to the kitchen to make a pot of coffee.

After the coffee brewed, I returned to the living room, and smiling, joined him on our couch.

As I sat down, he suddenly seemed to go berserk!

Without any forewarning, he grabbed me, pinned me against the back of the couch and began kissing me so roughly that I began to cry. I tried to push him away, but I could not.

He suddenly seemed to go berserk.

I was in trouble and I knew it! The more I resisted, the more frenzied he became. His face and hands began to take on a blotchy red color, and he started perspiring profusely. It was all too apparent what was going to happen.

There was no doubt in my mind that this man was going to be rough and punishing. The certainty of what was about to happen was paralyzing. However…as my fear escalated, some primitive instinct seemed to take over.

Suddenly, I quit fighting. My body has somehow turned itself off. I heard myself saying, in a voice that I didn't recognize, "My ex-husband will be bringing my children home at any minute. He is a big man with a vicious temper. He will *kill* you if he finds you here like this."

My attacker stopped dead in his tracks. Giving me a look that could have frozen over the gates of hell, he got up, grabbed his jacket and cap and stormed out of our living room.

When he reached our front door, he threw it open with such force that he shattered the leaded-glass windowpanes. I sat immobilized.

Several minutes passed. Suddenly the tears started, and within seconds, I had escalated into out-of-control sobbing.

When I look back on this incident, I am appalled! I find it difficult to believe that I could have been so naïve. I accepted an invitation to go out, alone, on the high seas with a man about whom I knew absolutely nothing.

The sad truth is this. During that tumultuous period of my life, I would probably have accepted an invitation from any well dressed, apparently successful man who showed an interest in me, I was so terrified of being alone.

All too often, frightened women respond in the way that I did. Occasionally, there are tragic consequences for this kind of cavalier disregard.

PLAYING THE GAME — AND WINNING

The game — as it is called — is like a mating dance in which the woman entices and the man pursues. Success or failure depends upon the woman. The paradox is, that in general, the less a woman does, the more successful she becomes. And like a skilled poker player, a smart woman does not show her hand.

BOUVIER

Many years ago, an article in Time Magazine quoted Black Jack Bouvier – Jacqueline Kennedy's father — as saying the following about his famous daughter:

"An attractive woman should be mysterious. Always holding something back to keep people guessing ... Jack (referring to President Kennedy) would take her to parties and then leave her alone while he 'worked the room.'

In response, she developed her famous, 'I'm-here-but-I'm-really-not-here' approach to the world.

More often than not, she answered questions with her dazzling smile — period."

That, ladies, is seduction. At its finest.

Jacqueline Bouvier's father, Black Jack, was a notorious womanizer who clearly understood that the more elusive a woman was the more intriguing she became.

Men are initially attracted to a woman if they find her intriguing. They are drawn to her mystery the way a moth is drawn to the flame. Therefore, any well groomed, nice looking, bright, pleasant-acting woman is capable of attracting the attention of men.

If a woman is smart enough to stand still and allow men to pursue her, she will quickly find herself inside the ballpark. The trick, though, is keeping a man's attention after you have gone out with him a few times.

Keeping a good man's attention is similar to that old homily about "the carrot and the donkey". The donkey keeps moving forward, because the carrot is always just slightly out reach. So, don't be too accommodating and don't pursue. Then watch men flock toward you.

REGARDING THE WORD NO

Most women understand that "no" means no. Men, however, hear the word "no" from a woman and consider it a challenge which only makes them try harder. Once a woman comprehends the effectiveness of a softly spoken "no," she will want to say it more often.

"No, I can't see you tonight."

You are not someone who is available at the last minute.

"No, I can't meet you halfway."

You know that a man should be picking you up.

"No, I can't accept this expensive gift".

Accepting expensive gifts creates obligation.

"No, I can't go away with you this weekend."

Not until we have a real commitment.

Nine out of ten times when women say "yes," they should be saying "no."

"NO! NO! NO! NO! NO!"

Believe it or not, success with dynamic and outstanding men is directly related to your adroit use of the word "no." When you say "no" remember to smile, because there is nothing as seductive as a warm and inviting smile.

SMILE! SMILE! SMILE! SMILE! SMILE!

A note to the attractive single woman. Do not expect upwardly mobile men to be at your beck and call simply because you are beautiful and good in bed. It takes more! There are hundreds of gorgeous, sexually-available women chasing after every dynamic man. Don't you become one of them.

CHASING ALWAYS HAS A BACKLASH

One of the most destructive things a woman can do is taking over before she has been invited to do so. There are so many subtle ways women do this. The most obvious way is chasing. Some women persist in chasing men even when experience proves beyond a shadow of a doubt this does not work. Women just can't seem to resist.

Take, for example, the following true story. This woman was newly divorced after a twenty-year marriage and still living in her large beach-front home in Malibu.

"I don't understand why men aren't asking me to go out. I know that I am intelligent and reasonably attractive. I am also world-traveled."

Being a woman of action, she registered with a discreet dating service, and within a few days, she received a call from a man who sounded both educated and cultured. He invited her to have lunch with him and suggested they meet at a local restaurant in Malibu.

"How thoughtful and well-bred," she thought.

The following day they met for lunch. She found him both charming and sophisticated. After a thoroughly delightful lunch, she began fantasizing about seeing him again, and more often.

As he was leaving, he thanked her for an enjoyable afternoon, but said nothing more.

She asked if she would be hearing from him. He simply smiled and said that he would call her.

Several days later he did indeed call. He explained that, although he enjoyed her company, he would not be seeing her again.

She told him she was terribly disappointed, because she thought they had a lot in common. He mumbled something she didn't understand and said good-by. True to his word he did not call again.

Finally she called him.

"I told him that I understood he was not romantically interested in me, but I hoped we could be friends." He agreed that would be nice.

When again she didn't hear from him, she called him and invited him to a charity gala for which she had tickets. He accepted. They attended the gala, and she told me that she was proud to introduce him as her escort.

At the end of the evening, he proved himself to be a thoughtful and skilled lover. After that they dated on-and-off for the next two years, but only when she called him.

"I finally stopped calling," she said, "but getting over him has been more painful than I care to admit, even to myself."

Momentary self-gratification takes your focus off the goal.

Unfortunately, this story is not only true, but somewhat typical.

The man in this story made it amply clear that he was not interested in a romantic liaison, but the woman persisted. Encounters like this almost always end in heartache. Since men want to lead, the smartest and safest thing for women to do is to let them lead. Men with high self-esteem will insist upon it, anyway.

THE QUESTIONS WOMEN ASK

The following questions came from a provocative young woman who is beautiful and charming, but was failing with men. You may have asked some of these questions yourself.

He stopped calling. What did I do wrong?

Is it possible you were too accommodating? Were you available at the last minute? Did you drive to his house? Have you fixed intimate dinners for two at your home? Did you spend hours on the phone? Did you talk about your problems? Dynamic men lose interest in women who are needy.

Isn't dating supposed to be fun? Isn't that what it's all about?

Dating, in and of its self can be lots of fun, if that's all you want. If, however, you are interested in capturing the heart of some dynamic fellow, you will need to become more serious minded.

Why does it matter when I have sex? When it's right it's right. Right?

Wrong! It is 'right' only after you have of a commitment. Men of value have to respect a woman before they allow themselves to fall in love. Strongly masculine men lose respect for women who say "yes" too soon, because they rightly assume she has said "yes" too often.

Don't I owe him something? After the money he has spent on me?

Yes! You owe him the pleasure of your company.

Why doesn't recreational sex lead to commitment?

It can lead to commitment, but not with a worthwhile man. Most alpha-type males lose respect for women who surrender too easily. Real men expect to work for what they get.

How do I let a man know how I want to be treated?

The most effective way of letting a man know what you want, and what you don't want, is by your actions. For instance: If he tells an off-color joke—don't laugh. If he arrives late—be gone. If he invites you to come to his house for dinner say, "No thank you."

How do I set boundaries without making a man feel controlled?

One of the best ways to set boundaries is non-verbally. As explained above, men feel controlled when women tell them "what" to do and "how" to do it. When you use non-verbal communication, you can express yourself without making demands.

Why does it matter if my house is clean and inviting? Why should it matter to him?

If you don't take care of your own things, he will assume you won't take care of his things.

In this day and age, why does an occasional swear word matter?

Successful men can choose, and they want women they can be proud of. Foul language suggests that you may not be the virtuous women he aspires to have in his life. When your date hears you swear he may change his mind about you. For one thing, he can no longer be certain that you won't use foul language in front of his family and his business acquaintances. (Little annoyances can turn into big issues.) A woman who resorts to profanity reveals a tendency toward anger. And remember, men want their woman to be an exemplar of superior womanhood.

What's wrong with wearing sexy clothes? They make me feel good.

You can wear any kind of clothes you want to wear as long as you understand what skimpy clothes imply. They imply sexual availability. Men of substance do not enjoy having other men ogle their women; these men are attracted to women who are more demure.

What's wrong with short skirts and tight sweaters? That's the style.

It may be the style, but you will attract more significant men if you dress more discreetly. Men see provocative clothing as synonymous with easy sex. That is not the image you want to project.

What's wrong with tank tops? Every woman wears them.

No, not every woman. Skimpy outfits are not worn by women of value who have high self-esteem.

Why does my personal hygiene matter so much? Men don't really notice things like that, do they?

Most men are acutely aware of a woman's personal hygiene. Men definitely notice if your hair is unwashed, your clothes un-pressed, or you have neglected to take a shower. Bad breath and body order kill ardor. These omissions are perilous.

How can the way I handle my money affect the type of men I attract? The man I date won't know how I handle my money.

Successful men have learned to read people. Besides, even in casual conversation, women reveal their attitudes about money. Since successful men have worked hard to get where they are, they want and need responsible partners. This holds true for men at all societal levels.

How does my driving affect the kind of man I will attract? How can that have anything to do with guys asking me out?

A woman's character is apparent when she is driving. The way she drives is reflective of her attitude toward others. A rude and careless driver is likely to be a rude and careless woman.

If I have a girlfriend who is a lush but he never meets her, how can that hurt?

Our secrets seep out in conversation. Besides, women of character do not have girlfriends who are lushes. A woman's speech and attitudes are colored by her acquaintances.

What's wrong with telling a lie now and then, after all he's not my father.

Lying is the equivalent of mortal sin when it comes to building a relationship. When the man you are dating discovers you have lied to him (and he will), trust goes out the window. Trust is an essential. One small lie cancels months of trust.

What is so wrong about discussing my family with the men I date?

It suggests that you are too closely tied to your family. Men are not interested in your family, at least not until after the relationship has becomes significant. If a man asks about your family, say as little as possible.

Why can't I include my children on dates? Shouldn't he get to know my kids?

This is a two part question: (a) It isn't fair to subject your children to the various men you are dating, and (b) a man should not be allowed to get involved with your children until he has decided to take you seriously. Only when you are confident of his intentions should he be given an opportunity to get close to your children. Children should not be used as pawns. It is not good for the children. It is not good for the relationship.

What is so wrong with giving advice? I'm good at it!

The man you are dating is (hopefully) not looking for a mother. If you are wrong, he will blame you. If you are right, he will resent you. When a woman instructs, she makes a man feel less like a man and more like a little boy.

Alcohol is what makes dating fun! If I have only a few drinks and don't get drunk, what's the harm?

Judgment is impaired when women drink alcohol; they tend to talk more and reveal more. They are more likely to end up saying "yes" when you should be saying "no".

I am not suggesting total abstinence, since that would be a bit unrealistic, but I am advising caution.

If it's right, it's right! So why does it matter when we have sex?

There is a big difference between lust and an expression of love through sexual union. Lust is self-gratifying and when it is over, it's over. Love, on the other hand, expressed through sexual giving-and-receiving can form a lasting bond between two people.

Isn't your view a bit old fashioned?

Probably! However, since 50% of all marriages end in divorce, a more cautious approach to sex is at least worth considering. Anyway, casual sex does not seem to be making a positive contribution in today's world.

You say a man can tell how promiscuous I am. How is that possible?

Women must wall-off their emotions in order to successfully engage in casual sex.   Doing this creates a defensiveness that makes women appear hard. Men identify this hardness as promiscuity. Substantial men reject such women, which further reinforces their feelings of inadequacy.

Why is reading the newspaper so important?

If you are hoping to marry a man whose feet are firmly planted on the ground, understand that he too is looking for a well grounded woman. A mature man stays abreast of the news and will want to discuss current events. When he realizes that he is talking with someone who doesn't know what's going on in the world, he may decide he is dealing with a child.

What has locking my doors and drawing my drapes got to do with catching the right man?

Thinking well of oneself is reflected in so many ways. Locking your doors and drawing your drapes is an indication of concern for your own well-being and the safety of those in your household. If you demonstrate carelessness with your family, he can hardly anticipate you will take good care of him and his family.

→ *What's wrong with inviting a man somewhere?*

If you do the inviting, you are pursuing. Strong men do not look upon this as a plus.

What's wrong with helping a man straighten up his house or going shopping with him?

Too much availability suggests neediness. A woman with a full life does not have time to straighten up a man's home, nor is she inclined to accompany him while he runs errands.

What's wrong with taking my car if he does most of the driving?

The unspoken message is that you are a caretaker and are willing to become his provider. Without realizing it, you are emasculating him.

What's wrong with including his kids on our dates? I like kids!

It is not appropriate for him to include his children. Would he include his children if he were having lunch with a business associate?

What's wrong with telling him my problems? That's what friends do.

He is not your friend. Not until he has asked you to become his wife. Talking about problems may push him away if he is still shopping. Successful men are looking for someone who will make their lives easier.

What's wrong with meeting a man half way?

As I have said, powerful men value most what they have to work for. If you make yourself too available, they will value you less.

What's wrong with discussing old relationships? Everyone does it when they get into a new relationship.

No! Everyone does not. Women with élan do not talk about their past relationships, or loved ones who have died. Doing so creates a barrier.

What's wrong with calling him? Isn't our relationship supposed to be between equals?

It is better if you wait for him to call you. Alpha males are intent upon pursuing their women. Even when a man says he wants an equal relationship and you should call him part of the time, don't believe him. He doesn't mean it. You can check this out with your father or your brother.

What's wrong with accepting last minute invitations? I like spontaneity.

If you say "yes" to last minute invitations, he will assume you have no life of your own. Immediately, you become less valuable.

What's wrong with kissing or even petting on the first date?

If you kiss and pet on your first date, the man you are dating will rightly assume this is something you have done before. Significant men do not want a woman every other man in town has succeeded with. Men don't like to think that their special woman is not so special.

You say dynamic men expect more from the women they date? What does this mean?

Dynamic men are looking for adult women. Highly desirable men have often suffered through previous relationships with beautiful trophy wives. Hence, most of them are determined not to make the same mistake twice.

What do you mean when you say dynamic men do a lot of testing?

When saying goodnight, they forget to mention that they would like to see you again.

They don't call for days after taking you out. (Don't even think of calling them.)

They suggest that you invite them to dinner at your house.

They push for immediate sex.

How can a man tell when a woman isn't really listening to him?

The same way *you* can tell when someone isn't really listening to you.

How will a man ever get to know me if he's only interested in talking about himself? If he's attracted to me, doesn't he want to get to know me?

First things first! In the beginning, men may want to talk mostly about themselves, but once they decide you are someone special, they will want to know all about you.

In the past, when I played hard to get, the guys went away.

Lucky you! Dependent little boys will always walk away, because they are looking for someone to take care of *them*. Responsible men, however, react positively to women who demand respect.

What makes a dynamic man eventually trust? What makes him want to commit?

Sought-after men look for consistency before they trust. It takes patience to earn the confidence of a dynamic man.

How can these men feel emotionally insecure when they are so successful and are being chased by countless women?

Good question! Men, who have been overly indulged in childhood, do not usually excel when they become adults. Therefore, it is safe to say that super-achievers have experienced some pain and disappointment while growing up. This kind of emotional insecurity lasts a life time. As for those women who chase men, they are not considered serious contenders.

You say dynamic men demand excellence from themselves and those around them. It sounds like he is going to be critical of me. Is this true?

Possibly! However, you are not likely to become a permanent part of such a man's life, unless you too are a high achiever. When dynamic men do commit, however, they often become a woman's greatest supporter.

Why doesn't a man who likes casual sex, think in terms of marriage with the woman he is having casual sex with?

Men who seek casual sex are usually enjoying a bit of R&R. But, yes, it is possible to end up married to a man with whom you have enjoyed casual sex. However, it is not likely that you will end up with a marriage made in heaven.

***You make the super-achieving man sound spoiled. Why
would I want him?***

If you are a nurturer, you won't mind if he is a little self-centered,
because he will also be a great provider and protector. But there is no
need for *you* to worry, because if you are not a caregiver, he won't choose
you.

THE WORDS YOU USE

The things we don't take care of, we lose. If we don't water our plants, they will die. If we don't lovingly attend to our pets, they will run away.

Women of value are thoughtful and considerate of others. However, sometimes even the best of women unknowingly say hurtful things. For instance, something as seemingly insignificant as a pronoun can make a big difference to a relationship.

"I"

I want to encourage you to use the pronoun "I", instead of the pronoun "we", when you are dating. If you absent-mindedly use the word "we" when talking about an ex-husband or an ex-boyfriend, you can offend a man who may be in the process of falling in love with you.

Are you always sensitive to a man's feelings? Men don't always show their feelings, but they have them just the same. Few things are as destructive to a new relationship as thoughtless remarks about ex-boyfriends and ex-husbands.

An insensitive woman says:

When *our* house burned to the ground, *we* had to live in a trailer for six months with *our* four children. It was a nightmare for *us*.

A more sensitive woman says:

When *my* house burned to the ground, *I* had to live in a trailer for six months with *my* four children. It was a nightmare for *me*.

When a woman talks about what "we" used to do and where "we" used to go, she unknowingly erects a wall which can eventually become a relationship breaker.

There are both constructive and destructive ways of saying things. All men find the constructive ways much more appealing.

Destructive: My ex-husband and I are still very close.

He thinks: Oh, no, they're still emotionally attached!

Constructive: My ex and I stay on good terms because of our children.

He thinks: Seems reasonable.

Destructive:	My ex frequently fails to make child support payments.
He thinks:	Will I have to assume financial responsibility for his children?
Constructive:	My ex doesn't have much money, but he cares about his children.
He thinks:	Good.

Destructive:	My teenage daughter is driving me crazy.
He thinks:	I don't want to live with the teenager from hell.
Constructive:	I have a teenager and she is pretty much ok.
He thinks:	Great.

Destructive:	My parents are not religious.
He thinks:	Are they spiritually bankrupt?
Constructive:	My parents are very spiritual. (It isn't necessary to explain that they are not active in church or synagogue.)
He thinks:	OK.

Destructive:	I'm so busy I don't have time to read the paper.
He thinks:	Am I dating a self-indulgent child?
Constructive:	I watch the news on TV in the morning.
He thinks:	Good. A woman I can talk to about current events.

Destructive:	I have to be really careful or I gain weight.
He thinks:	Oh no! Is she going to get fat?
Constructive:	Say nothing about your weight!
He thinks:	At last… a woman who doesn't carry-on about her weight.

Destructive:	Do you find me attractive?
He thinks:	She's fishing. She's too needy!
Constructive:	I think the content of a person's character is more important than the way they look.
He thinks:	Ah ha, a grown-up.

Destructive:	My father thinks I'm stupid.
He thinks:	Uh, oh…probably has issues with men.
Constructive:	My father is a man with very strong opinions.
He thinks	I have strong opinions myself.

Destructive:	My father is leaving his entire estate to his second wife.
He thinks:	Why is she telling me this?
Constructive:	I am so happy that Daddy has finally found someone nice.
He thinks:	What a lovely woman.

Destructive:	My sister and I tell each other everything.
He thinks:	Oh no, they'll talk about how well I perform in bed.
Constructive:	My sister and I are close.
He thinks:	Cool.

Destructive:	My brother is a self-centered brat. We don't speak.
He thinks:	Uh, oh…
Constructive:	My brother is very successful, but we aren't close.
He thinks:	Too bad.

Destructive:	My mom hates my dad.
He thinks:	Great, another messed-up family.
Constructive:	My mom remarried and we like her husband. (No need to explain that mom was married four times before she got it right.)
He thinks:	A close family. I like that.

Destructive:	I have trouble making ends meet.
He thinks:	Is she looking to be rescued?
Constructive:	My living standard has been scaled back but I'm doing fine.
He thinks:	I like this woman, she can manage well.

Destructive:	My apartment is like an oven in the summer.
He thinks:	Why is she telling me this?
Constructive:	My apartment is small, but I love it.
He thinks:	I like a woman who is content with what she has.

Destructive:	I know I should help my kids with their homework, but they are always watching television.
He thinks:	An immature women with spoiled brat kids.
Constructive:	I try to help my children with homework although sometimes it's hard to find the time.
He thinks:	Sounds like a good Mom.

Destructive:	I take my children with me everywhere I go.
He thinks:	Oh no, enmeshed with her kids.
Constructive:	I love my children, but sometimes it's nice to get away from them.
He thinks:	My kind of woman!

Destructive:	I hate to cook.
He thinks:	I hate TV dinners!
Constructive:	Most of the time I cook very simple meals.
He thinks:	That's fine with me.

Destructive:	I hate watching football and basketball.
He thinks:	I love football and basketball!
Constructive:	Football and basketball are interesting, but I wish I had someone who could help me understand them better.
He thinks:	Cool! I can do that.

Destructive:	Do you love me?
He thinks:	Another desperate woman: I'm out of here.
Constructive:	I have fun when I'm with you, you're good company.
He thinks:	I'm in love!

Your choice of words is more important than you think. The next time you are out with a man, be especially mindful of "what" you are saying and "how" you are saying it. If you heed the examples I have just given you, it won't take long before some sought-after man realizes that you are a very special woman...perhaps the very woman he has been searching for.

THE WORK REQUIRED FOR SUCCESS

O ur thoughts mold our destinies. Thoughts are the bricks we use to build our lives. We become what we think about.

Therefore, if I think I am poor, and I expect to stay

poor, guess what? I'll probably always be poor! Why? Because every thought we think comes back to us.

When I first began my own downhill spiral, I was so miserable I could think of nothing but my desperation. At that time, I had no clothes, no family I could turn to for support, no money and an old car. At 41 years of age, I thought I was 'over-the-hill'.

I thought my life was over!

But, fate had other plans for me.

A Greater Power sent a woman into my life who became my mentor. One of my new teacher's first instructions was that every time a negative thought crossed my mind, I was to say *"cancel-cancel"*, and say it out loud.

Obviously, she didn't understand who I was!

Why, when I was in high school, hadn't I been May Day Queen? And when I went off to college, hadn't I gone through College Rush and received bids from every sorority on campus?—something that had never before been done. And in addition, hadn't I been invited to join the Junior League even though we were dirt poor? Oh yes! I was a big deal in my own mind! Therefore, someone like me couldn't go about muttering *"cancel-cancel"*.

What is her secret?

But, as it turned out, I not only could—but did! As my emotional pain progressed, I started saying *"cancel-cancel"* to my every negative thought. Strangely, saying this really helped me. I became more positive. I may have still been *circling the drain*, but at least I had become teachable.

Cancel - cancel

THE POWER OF POSITIVE THINKING

Martin Luther King said, "I have a dream" and then held fast to his vision and changed the destiny of an entire race of people.

There is great power in being passionately focused. My personal belief is that the more intensely I focus, the more certainly I will bring it to pass. I have actually experienced the results of the power of positive thinking a dozen times in my life.

After Peter jilted me — remember Peter? — I was crazy with anger, fear and humiliation. I had no money, no family and only a few friends, so I prayed to lie down and never get back up. In the meantime, I had to find a job.

She penned a letter to God describing the man she was longing for.

How could I find a job in my present state? I was a walking nightmare: I looked like warmed-over death. I had no decent clothes and I was frighteningly thin and claustrophobic. And I had never in my life held down a full-time job. I sat down with a felt-tipped pen and penned a request to the God I didn't really believe in. I would like to share my letter with you.

Heavenly Father ~ I'm so scared. I must find work. I need your help and I hope you will help me. I need a secretarial job that is no more than ten minutes from our apartment, because my car is very old. And I must make a top salary in order to meet our expenses. In addition, I need to sit near a window, because I am so claustrophobic. Also, I have to be able to wear casual clothes, because I have no dress clothes left. Thank you. With much love. ~

Jade

I had been told by three different employment agencies that there were no secretarial jobs available at the salary that I needed. However, in the ensuing six months, I landed *six* different jobs that all met my basic requirements.

I got fired from the first five jobs. Each time I got fired within weeks of being hired. I was such an emotional wreck I couldn't concentrate. Each time I got fired, I would take a deep breath and gird myself up to go out and get yet another job. On my last job, I lasted seven months. Then…my present husband asked me to marry him.

This is a true story.

I credit my change of fortune to a desperation which made me teachable. I also give credit to my grandfather (a Christian minister), to the mature women who came into my life and to the philosophy of positive thinking that we currently refer to as The Secret.

REWARDS OF SELF-SUFFICIENCY

Self-esteem is the by-product of self-sufficiency. When a woman with high self-esteem finds herself in an abusive relationship, she is able to say: "If you don't start treating me with more consideration, I'm leaving." Then, if the man in her life doesn't apologize, she has the strength to leave.

You can have whatever your heart desires.

"How do women do this?" you ask. "How do they walk away?"

If a woman has established a successful life of her own, she knows that happiness does not depend upon having a man. She wants a man, but she doesn't need a man. The reason one woman can insist on respect, while another woman is too frightened to do so is all about personal self-esteem.

The woman who has built a suitable life of her own knows she will continue to prosper with or without a man. Paradoxically…these are the women who walk down the aisle with the very man every other woman wants.

If you are one of those women who have not yet put it together with the right man, now is the time to take stock. Winning the heart of a man of value is hard work, but careful attention to detail will bring delightful results.

THE FACTS — SAD BUT TRUE

Let's focus on the subject of marriage. One of the most common problems women cope with is not attracting—and not being able to hold on to—a man of high caliber.

Even a gorgeous woman with an, "I don't have to work on me" attitude is probably going to be disappointed if she has dreams of marrying an orthopedic surgeon. If the orthopedic surgeon she has in mind is successful, and most surgeons who stay in practice *are* successful, he will not be seriously attracted to a "there is nothing wrong with me" woman.

Now! He may take this woman out, have sex with her, bestow gifts on her, even take her on interesting trips, but he probably will not often offer to share his last name with her.

But let's be very clear about one thing. It is possible to be a stay-at-home-mom or a working mother-with-children, and be as accomplished as any orthopedic surgeon. Accomplished people are people who have applied themselves wholeheartedly to any task in which they find themselves. I, on the other hand, had never bothered to apply myself. I was always more interested in having fun.

After my nervous breakdown, the woman who subsequently became my mentor encouraged me to start making my bed *every* single morning. After I recovered from this challenging assignment, she then told me to start washing my car once a week.

"Are you kidding? That piece of junk?" I responded.

"Yes," she said. "Because when you take care of the things the Universe has bestowed upon you, it will give you more. Well! I certainly did not believe that! However, I needed and valued her friendship, so I began making my bed and washing my car (by hand). I couldn't afford to take my car to a car wash. Today, I drive a luxury car. And today I can have any car my heart desires.

I attribute my good fortune to taking good care of the gifts life provided me, as life provided them. But, my success isn't the result of good luck. I worked hard for the life I have today.

We are in control of our own lives.

After faithfully washing my old car every week, I began to notice that I was feeling better. As my life continued to improve, I slowly began to incorporate these principles into all areas of my life. Almost imperceptibly, I arrived at the enviable life I have today.

WE CAN ATTRACT ONLY WHO WE ARE

Women who have the most successful lives are women who have become attuned to the laws of nature. For example, an emotionally healthy woman who comes from a middle class background, and has had only a high school education, doesn't aspire to marry a United States Senator.

An individuated woman would welcome into her life a man with background, achievements, and ethics similar to her own. Such emotionally healthy women get married, have families and become solid parts of their community. The less fortunate woman is the one who decides she must have a high-income husband, but does not have a personal life that will attract such a man.

If you are hoping to marry a man who is hard working, constant, devoted to family, and professionally successful, you must become an exemplar of the life you want.

Like attracts like.

Therefore, if you are unsatisfied with the man you are currently dating, you need to first concentrate on getting your own life in tip-top order! Once that task is completed, the universe will take care of finding you the right man. Once you address yourself to changing the errors you have been making in your life, dynamic men will suddenly appear from out of nowhere.

A BETTER GAME PLAN

If you are a woman beyond the age of thirty and you want to get married—perhaps again—you probably need to rethink your game plan. You may need to begin doing the exact opposite of what you have been doing.

If you are interested in finding a man of substance, it is important to remember, that his life style is different from that of the ordinary men. These men are effective across many levels and they look for very special women. The women they choose must stand out from the rest.

Regardless of a man's monetary status, dynamic men with lots of testosterone want responsible women. Outstanding men want women who are exemplary. When a self-assured man sees a woman he wants, nothing will stop him. And, it doesn't take him long to make up his mind! Strong men are natural hunters and warriors.

THOSE GOING NOWHERE RELATIONSHIPS

If you have been dating a man for longer than six months—and he still isn't talking about marriage—your chances of having a committed relationship are very slim. The question then becomes: What should you do when you find yourself in a situation like this?

Issuing an ultimatum and then changing your mind is tantamount to committing emotional suicide. Be certain that getting "out" is what you really want, because there is nothing more destructive than saying, "I'm leaving!" and then not leaving.

Do I want to spend the rest of my life with this man?

A woman can never regain her advantage, once she has threatened and not followed through. When a man realizes a woman is not strong enough to "mean" what she says, he will then take even more undue advantage. This kind of discounting can turn into abuse.

There are only two viable choices. 1) Leave him. 2) Start working on yourself. You may be doing something wrong if the man you are seeing does not want a permanent relationship. Have you been smothering him? Are you clinging too tightly? Have you tried to take control?

HIS NAME WAS WALLY

We met at a cocktail party. He was drop-dead gorgeous and had an air of self-confidence that was absolutely irresistible.

After saying "hello" he looked me directly in the eye, smiled broadly and said, "You look like seven generations of Pasadena money!"

Then...as though he had known me all of his life, he asked if I would have lunch with him the following day.

I accepted, of course.

Wally said he would come for me about noon.

Beware, when you hear 'about noon.' That is a red flag. It means you aren't very important to him. It means, "I'll get there any time I feel like it."

The next day I was ready and waiting at 12:00 sharp.

12:00 came and went. Then 12:10, 12:20, 12:25. No Wally!

This apparent casual disregard was counter to all that my mother had taught me about men. It made me furious!

I decided to give "Mr. Self-Assured" something to think about. I told my teenage daughters, who were home at the time, that when my erstwhile date showed up, they were to tell him (via our apartment intercom) that I had waited until 12:30 and then I had gone shopping, and I left.

When I returned from my dreamed-up shopping trip, my daughters were fibrillating with excitement. They

Wally was aghast!

said that Wally buzzed our apartment at exactly 12:40, and when they told him I had gone shopping, he kept repeating,

"I don't believe this! I just don't believe this!"

That evening Wally called me on the phone and demanded, in an accusatory tone of voice, that I explain. I told him that I had waited thirty minutes, and then assuming he wasn't coming, I had left.

Don't wait around: If he's late, leave.

He was aghast!

Nevertheless, he asked me again to go out with him, and we dated for several months. He was never again late, but this man was not the one for me.

By taking decisive action, I risked losing, but the good news is I didn't. Previous experience had already taught me that self-assured men are not deterred by challenge.

By demonstrating personal self-esteem, I got this man's attention. Then I was able to set boundaries. We dated long enough for me to decide that it was I (not he) who was no longer interested.

THE QUESTIONNAIRE

This section is designed to help you identify the things in your life that you may be overlooking. Please consider each section carefully. There are questions at the end of each section. Answer these questions and decide where you need to make changes.

You may want to answer them again in three months.

Give yourself points according to the following:

> Always = 4 points
>
> Usually = 3 points
>
> Occasionally = 2 points
>
> Hardly Ever = 1 point

YOUR PERSONAL HYGIENE SPEAKS VOLUMES

Some women don't realize the importance of personal hygiene. But the fact is that an average-looking woman who is fastidious is far more intriguing to a dynamic male than a beauty who is careless about her hygiene.

Remember, men don't miss a thing!

Meticulous grooming is an essential. Scuffed shoes, chipped polish, poor dental hygiene, dirty hair, wrinkled clothing, clinging dog or cat hairs are all critical grooming errors and speak volumes about who a woman is.

Attention to detail carries the day.

Years ago, I had an opportunity to watch the filming of a movie starring Elizabeth Taylor. As I watched, I was mesmerized by the attention given to even the smallest of details. Just as attention to detail is vital when making a mega-movie, attention to detail is an imperative for a woman trying to market herself.

As you know, you get only one chance to make a good first impression.

MY HYGIENE

	Today	Later
I bathe at least once a day. *yes*	4	
I shampoo my hair regularly. *yes*	4	
My nails are carefully manicured. *yes*	3	
I visit my dry cleaner regularly. —	4	
My undergarments are always fresh. *yes*	4	
The scent of my perfume does not overtake a room. *yes*	4	
I apply makeup sparingly. *yes*	4	
Total	27	
Divide by 7 to get your net score	3.8	

❖ Most women bathe at least once a day. But some women do not consider it necessary to bathe before going from the office on to a dinner date. Bathing is a must, even if it means postponing dinner until a later hour.

❖ Since fastidiousness represents femininity, you should consider shampooing daily if you don't already do this. Freshly shampooed hair is alluring. Oily, stringy or matted hair is off-putting.

❖ Men notice three-day-old manicures. If you can't arrange a fresh manicure before joining him for dinner, the next best thing is to remove your polish and apply a coat of quick-drying clear polish.

❖ Blouses that need to be dry-cleaned should be taken to the cleaners after every wearing. Freshness is an imperative.

❖ Panties and bras must always be absolutely fresh, more so than outer garments. Body odor accumulates instantly on underclothing. If you cannot get home to change before a date, put a fresh pair of underwear in your purse in a zip lock bag. You will then have an air-tight place to store your soiled things after you have changed.

❖ Better to wear no perfume than wear too much. Remember: "A a little dab will do you."

❖ No woman, not even a very young woman, looks appealing with too much make-up. Once over thirty, women must, absolutely must, wear less and less make up to be appealing.

YOUR WARDROBE TELLS A STORY

The clothes you wear tell a story about you and about the importance you place on the date. If you wear worn-out jeans, a cotton shirt and scuffed shoes, your clothes tell one story. If you wear freshly pressed black pants, a silk blouse, a black jacket and highly polished leather flats, this tells another story. If you dress halfway between these two extremes it tells yet another story.

The main aspects of allure are: neat, clean, and well pressed. There is something delectably feminine about a woman who is freshly dressed.

Clothing that is too revealing or too low-cut sends the wrong message. It says, "I doubt you will be impressed with the rest of me, so I am going to emphasize my body!"

Sophisticated women know the difference between arousing a man sexually and simply intriguing him. Discriminating women want to intrigue, not arouse. Too-tight and too low-cut clothing is sexually suggestive. There is a huge difference between a street hooker and an elegantly groomed matron.

Understated clothing brings the kind of attention substant women seek, and sophistication can be achieved with a few well-chosen outfits. A basic wardrobe might be:

- ❖ A good black dress – not too short
- ❖ One well-cut pantsuit
- ❖ A stylish pair of heels
- ❖ A good pair of flats
- ❖ A good bag
- ❖ Several nice blouses
- ❖ Pressed jeans

MY DRESS CODE	Today	Later
I do not wear skirts that are too short.	_____	_____
I never wear pants that are tight fitting.	_____	_____
My sweaters are not snug.	_____	_____
I avoid tank tops and bare midriffs.	_____	_____
I do not wear four inch heels.	_____	_____
My jeans are always clean and pressed.	_____	_____
Total	_____	_____
Divide by 6 to get your net score	_____	_____

- ❖ Short-short skirts may be adorable on teenagers, but on older women, these skirts shout easy and available. Not a message *you* want to send.

❖ Too-tight pants may attract men with a roving eye, but substantial men will not become seriously interested. Too-tight pants on older women indicate lack of breeding.

❖ Men of substance are looking for life-partners, not just quick and easy lays.

❖ Tank tops and bare midriffs are cute on teenage girls, but older women who wear tank tops and bare midriffs are trying to reclaim their lost youth. There is nothing more unattractive than an older woman trying to look like a teenager.

❖ Tight fitting sweaters fall into the same category as short-short skirts and too-tight pants. And, high school kids have a name for four-inch heels: they laugh and call them "fuck-me" pumps.

❖ Women of any age can wear clean and freshly pressed jeans with élan. Certainly, women in their thirties, forties and fifties are attractive and appropriately dressed in properly cared for jeans.

WOMEN WHO LISTEN

Have you ever wondered when you see an only-average-looking woman with an outstanding and gorgeous man? What does he sees in her? It may be that the average-looking woman knows how to listen. An average woman who listens well is far more attractive than her stunning, but self-centered counterpart.

Do you know that the more you encourage a man to talk about himself, the more intriguing *you* become? I will give you an example.

After I had divorced my children's father, a good-looking man that I was attracted to invited me to have dinner with him.

The first half of the evening went smoothly enough, but after dinner he simply stopped talking. As the silence dragged on, I grew more and more uncomfortable.

In desperation I finally said, "You have such powerful hands." To my utter amazement, my date suddenly started talking again.

Apparently, even successful and intimidating grown men can be uncomfortable on a first date. I guess that after they have invited you, made the reservations, picked you up and opened all of your doors, they can fizzle out. Sometimes even seemingly self-assured men may need a bit of encouragement.

Anyway…my date started talking again after I had commented on his hands. Before the evening was over, this man had told me about his childhood in a small mid-western town, about the pressures of owning his own business, about his frustration on the golf course, and even a few things about the problems he was having with his teenage sons.

I was dumbfounded as I sat there listening. This man's willingness to talk had seemingly materialized from out of nowhere. How had a simple remark about *hands* brought on the story of his life?

At the end of our evening together, as he was saying goodnight, he looked me in the eyes and tenderly told me that he thought I was one of the most intriguing women he had ever met. Huh? I had said almost *nothing* all evening!

Success comes with asking questions, making positive comments. Knowing how to listen is a skill. Knowing how to listen with real interest is a profound skill.

MY LISTENING SKILLS	Today	Later
I try to resist talking too much even when I'm nervous.	_____	_____
I avoid criticizing, arguing or giving advice.	_____	_____
I stop myself from interrupting.	_____	_____
I always maintain eye contact.	_____	_____
I listen attentively.	_____	_____
I ask appropriate questions about what he is talking about.	_____	_____
I concentrate on staying interested in what my date is saying.	_____	_____
Total	_____	_____
Divide by 7 to get your net score	_____	_____

Women sometimes cover up their nervousness with non-stop talking. If you have a tendency to over-talk, try to concentrate on being absolutely quiet. Better to say nothing than to say too much.

When a man asks you to have dinner with him, he is anticipating a pleasant evening with an attractive woman. The last thing men want to do is spend time with an opinionated, self-absorbed ball-buster.

Maintaining eye contact is another good thing to do. It indicates that you are really paying attention. A woman who listens carefully makes a man feel important. It also helps him fall in love!

Asking questions shows a man that you really care about what he is saying. What man can resist this kind of attention? Most men say sex doesn't compare to a woman who knows how to listen to him. Listening is the coup de grace of seduction.

YOUR VOICE AND HOW YOU USE IT

Some women swear.

Some laugh too loudly.

Some talk incessantly.

These unfeminine characteristics are a turn-off. The tone and quality of a woman's voice, in addition to what she is saying, sends a definite message.

Are you sending the right message?

MY SPEECH	Today	Later
I speak softly. *sometime*	_____	_____
I keep myself from gushing and giggling. *?*	_____	_____
I speak slowly and distinctly. *fast*	_____	_____
I refrain from swearing (at least in *never* public)	_____	_____
Total	_____	_____
Divide by 4 to get your net score	_____	_____

❖ Wealthy parents spend fortunes sending their daughters to finishing schools where their darlings are taught appropriate social skills, among which is how to speak properly. These young women are taught to lower their voices, clearly pronounce their words and speak slowly.

❖ The reason wealthy parents send their daughters to finishing schools is to prepare them for an upper-level life style. When a woman speaks slowly and distinctly, it is apparent that she has been carefully reared. Since water seeks its own level, this behavior attracts men who have also been given cultural advantages which will enable them to succeed.

❖ Using expletives indicates lack of refinement, as well as a lack of an adequate vocabulary. Whereas, a soft voice invites intimacy.

YOUR HOME SPEAKS VOLUMES

When a man enters your home for the first time, he learns more about you than he will learn in the next six months of dating you. Your home is a looking glass into your soul. It reveals everything about you.

A clean and orderly house speaks of care and responsibility and translates into femininity. On the other hand, a messy house bespeaks of laziness, not a trait one wants to advertise.

An inviting home will have:

❖ Soft throw pillows — which suggest warmth and comfort.

❖ Pretty guest towels — which express charm as well as consideration for visitors.

❖ Scented candles — hinting of femininity.

❖ Fresh flowers — always synonymous with femininity.

❖ Interesting magazines — portraying intelligent activity.

❖ Family photographs — illustrating a well integrated life.

❖ Soft music and subdued lighting — very romantic.

❖ A well used fireplace — cozy and inviting.

MY HOME	Today	Later
My home is always clean and orderly.	_____	_____
My carpet is thoroughly vacuumed.	_____	_____
I have books and magazines on my coffee table.	_____	_____
I have fresh flowers and plants in my home.	_____	_____
My kitchen is spotless.	_____	_____
My bathrooms are clean and fresh.	_____	_____
My beds are always made.	_____	_____
The lighting in my home is adequate but subdued.	_____	_____
I have attractive pictures on the walls.	_____	_____
I have only a few photographs of family members.	_____	_____
Total	_____	_____
Divide by 10 to get your net score	_____	_____

❖ Your home paints a telling picture. It is not enough to have things attractively arranged. Your house or apartment must also be clean and well kept. How can you have a lovely and inviting home if your carpets are not thoroughly vacuumed?

❖ Interesting magazines and books on your coffee table make your home come to life.

❖ Potted plants and flowers are a lovely touch. (Joan Crawford, for instance, who was reputed to have been a cruel and uncaring woman, had only artificial flowers in her mansion. It is alleged she did not want to be bothered watering live plants.)

❖ A spotless kitchen says volumes about the woman who cooks in it.

❖ Bathrooms and sex are similar in some respects. A woman whose bathroom is less than sparklingly fresh may also be a bit haphazard about feminine hygiene. On the other hand, a woman with a fresh and attractive bathroom will probably also be fastidious about hygiene, therefore more sexually appealing. There does seem to be a connection.

❖ Making your bed first thing in the morning sets your mood for the rest of the day. It is also a positive statement about the person who sleeps in the bed.

❖ Subdued lighting suggests peacefulness. Peace is something successful men dream of finding. Need I say more?

❖ Attractive pictures turn a house or apartment into a home.

❖ Do not to have gazillions of family photographs about. Be circumspect when it comes to your family. Yes, you have one. Yes, you love them. But there should be only a few family photographs about.

MONEY MANAGEMENT AND MATURITY

Women who do not manage money well are usually less than mature. I have never known a woman who was irresponsible with money who was successful with alpha-type males.

Women who spend money foolishly may attract good looking little boys, but they usually do not end up with successful adult men. A woman's attitude toward money is a reflection of her level of maturity.

MY MONEY	Today	Later
I live within my means.	_____	_____
I pay my full monthly balance due on my credit cards.	_____	_____
I put money into my savings or investment account each month.	_____	_____
I balance my checkbook every month.	_____	_____
I carry adequate health and automobile insurance.	_____	_____
I refrain from buying-on-time and borrowing money.	_____	_____
Total	_____	_____
Divide by 6 to get your net score	_____	_____

❖ Living within your means says that you are a responsible adult. This sends the message you want to send. Remember: when a man asks you to become his wife, he recognizes that you are going to be managing *his* money.

❖ Paying off credit card balances each month is another indication of maturity. If the man you are dating sees that you manage your money, he will extrapolate that you will probably be able to manage his money.

❖ Part of being a responsible adult is being able to *save* money. What matters is that at least some amount is put aside each month. Saving is a discipline.

- ❖ Balancing one's checkbook is another indication of maturity. A college girl who balances her checkbook each month will probably marry well.

- ❖ Health insurance and automobile insurance indicate responsibility. If you were a successful man and could chose from twenty women, wouldn't you choose the most responsible woman you could find?

- ❖ Young men are driven by testosterone. Mature men are governed more by logic. Buying on credit or borrowing money from family members is not something grown-ups do. Adults do not pretend that they can afford what they cannot! A credit card that you pay in-full each month is, of course, acceptable.

- ❖ Impulse shopping? What woman hasn't indulged in impulse shopping? However, compulsive-obsessive shopping is a destructive habit and needs to be closely monitored.

YOUR FRIENDS ARE A REFLECTION

When people develop close friendships, they generally choose people similar to themselves. Do you have any hidden friendships? Friendships of which you are not proud? In order to feel good about yourself, it is important to associate with people of high caliber. I urge you to be scrupulously honest when answering the following questions.

MY FRIENDS

	Today	Later
I admire my friends.	_____	_____
I am not ashamed to introduce them to my family.	_____	_____
My friends work hard and are making significant contributions.	_____	_____
They are law-abiding.	_____	_____
They do not smoke, drink excessively or do drugs.	_____	_____
Total	_____	_____
Divide by 5 to get your net score	_____	_____

❖ Having respectable friends is important. We tend to pattern our attitudes and behaviors after those with whom we associate. In fact, we are who we associate with! Study your closest friends and discover who you are.

❖ If you feel comfortable introducing your friends to your family, you have undoubtedly chosen your friends well.

ALCOHOL – ONE MAY BE ONE TOO MANY

We all know that alcohol alters everyone's judgment and lowers inhibitions. Consequently…no intelligent woman would think of having a drink *before* going on a job interview. Nor would she drink during an interview.

So…why do women drink before going out on a date? And why do they think nothing of having several more drinks during the course of the evening? Isn't getting the man you want just as important as getting the job you want?

The average woman can probably handle one glass of wine without it seriously affecting her judgment. But for most women, more than one glass of alcohol will have an adverse effect on decision-making and deportment.

Women tend to talk more when drinking. They also tend to share intimacies they would not otherwise share; they do things they would not otherwise do. If you drink and date, you are more likely to say "yes" when you should be saying "no".

ALCOHOL	Today	Later
When dating, I limit myself to one drink per evening.	_____	_____
I am careful never to leave my drink unattended.	_____	_____
I do not drink before a date.	_____	_____
Total	_____	_____
Divide by 3 to get your net score	_____	_____

❖ If you feel you must drink, think about having only one drink per evening. This will allow you to better keep your wits about you.

❖ Most women are aware of the date rape drug Rohypnol or GHB, which is colorless, odorless and tasteless. But many women think that date rape could never happen to them. However, unless you really know the man you are with, you are wise to be cautious. You might not recognize the danger signs.

- ❖ It is tempting to take the edge-off with a drink. Don't do it! Your date will be able to tell.
- ❖ Having alcohol on your breath speaks volumes about *who* you are. Since alcohol can be so destructive, please be cautious about drinking and dating.

THOSE EXTRA POUNDS MATTER

Some women think extra pounds don't really matter. Other women think weight is the be-all and end-all of who they are. Weight does matter, but not as much as many women think.

Although it is true that most men are attracted to women who are thin, extra weight is not so much of a deterrent as being out of shape. Working out regularly is really important, because men will overlook extra weight if a woman is fit.

YOUR WEIGHT	Today	Later
My weight is within a healthy range.	_____	_____
I work out regularly.	_____	_____
I watch my intake of fat and sugar.	_____	_____
I drink a lot of water.	_____	_____
Total	_____	_____
Divide by 4 to get your net score	_____	_____

- ❖ Bone-thin should not be your goal. Being in a healthy range is what you want to strive for.
- ❖ If you have a bit of a weight problem, become more aware of the fat content of the food you eat.
- ❖ Drinking water is an imperative for weight control. Water improves the complexion as well as helping maintain weight. Also, did you know that even mild dehydration can cause depression?

YOUR DRIVING REVEALS YOUR TRUE SELF

What kind of driver are you? Do you display undesirable aspects of your character when driving? When behind the wheel of your car:

- ❖ Do you fail to buckle up?

- ❖ Do you refuse to yield?

- ❖ Do you ever become hostile or rude to other drivers?

- ❖ Do you use your horn as a weapon?

- ❖ Do you curse other drivers?

- ❖ Do you weave in and out of traffic?

- ❖ Do you drive too fast?

- ❖ Do you tailgate?

- ❖ What about the up-keep of your car?

- ❖ Do you take it to the car wash weekly?

- ❖ Do you take it in for regular checkups?

- ❖ Do you keep the inside neat and orderly?

When a man notices that you have a dirty and unkempt car it is a negative that he will stow away in his mind. Your objective when husband-hunting should be to illicit as few mental demerits as possible. An old car that is well kept makes a better impression than a dirty new car.

MY AUTOMOBILE	Today	Later
I buckle up.	_____	_____
I am courteous to other drivers.	_____	_____
I do not allow myself to race through yellow lights.	_____	_____
I take my car to the car wash each week (or wash it myself).	_____	_____
I have adequate automobile insurance.	_____	_____
My car is free of bumper stickers and decals.	_____	_____
My trunk and glove compartment are clean and orderly.	_____	_____
I pay parking tickets promptly.	_____	_____
I lock my car when I leave it.	_____	_____
I drive non-aggressively.	_____	_____
Total	_____	_____
Divide by 10 to get your net score	_____	_____

❖ Mature adults obey the law, and the law clearly states that we are to buckle up whenever a car is in motion.

❖ Courtesy is not something that can be put on and taken off. Courteousness and gentility are closely related and are sought-after qualities (whether consciously or unconsciously) by successful men who are looking for life-time partners.

❖ As tempting as it may be to race through an intersection before the light changes, stable adults do not race through yellow lights.

❖ Your car's appearance is a statement about you. Don't collect avoidable demerits from your newest *catch* just because you forget to visit the car wash.

❖ When you see another driver tailgating, what does that tell you? Doesn't it say the driver is impatient and heedless of the safety of others?

❖ All responsible people have automobile insurance.

❖ Bumper stickers and decals may be appropriate on a teenager's car, but noteworthy men are not looking to connect with teenyboppers.

❖ Although your trunk and glove compartments are not visible, personal power comes from knowing that all aspects of your life are in good working order.

❖ Adults pay parking tickets promptly. Paying parking tickets is one more thing that separates winners from losers.

❖ Women, who do not accept responsibility for their lives, usually do not end up happily married.

❖ An aggressive driver is saying, "Get out of my way!"

CAREER WOMEN MUST WEAR TWO HATS

The women I counseled in my practice were mostly successful in their careers. But none of these women were succeeding with men. They were in fact failing miserably. I found, after years of working with women that the characteristics that worked so well career-wise were often the most serious stumbling blocks when they were dating quality men.

When successful woman enters into a relationship with a top-notch man, she must learn to curb her competitive instincts if she hopes to succeed with him.

Too often, dynamic women end up with dependent men. Why? Because dependent men allow women to remain in control. However, such liaisons are usually not successful over the long haul.

Is it possible for a dynamic, super-capable woman to succeed with a strong, confident adult male? Yes! But it requires finesse and discipline on the part of the successful woman.

It is quite understandable that after spending a full day being forthright (a quality essential for business and professional success), most women will find it daunting to shift gears. However, it is to their ultimate advantage if they will do so.

Smashingly successful women must switch hats when dating. A woman must be able to move from a position of authority into a position of guest. She must learn to shift out of the leadership role into the role of follower. At least temporarily! Only one person can be the leader. Truly outstanding men will insist on having that role.

MY CAREER	Today	Later
I leave my career at the office.	_____	_____
I schedule adequate time for recreation.	_____	_____
I have time for family and friends.	_____	_____
My career is not the only important thing in my life today.	_____	_____
I try to be less assertive when I am dating.	_____	_____
Total	_____	_____
Divide by 5 to get your net score	_____	_____

❖ It is important not to talk about your career. If you are totally focused on your career, he will rightly assume that your career is one of the most important things in your life. This will not be acceptable to a man who comes from a position of success himself. These men insist on being number one in a women's life.

❖ A man may be impressed when he discovers that you are a successful career woman, but he will not respond positively if he senses that your career is inordinately important to you. You must give him the impression that you think he is number one, without saying so.

❖ If a man sees that you don't make time for your own family and friends, he will conclude that you won't have time for his family and friends. And, he will probably be right.

❖ Men of value are leaders and they will assume the leadership role. Therefore, it is important to find more subtle ways of communicating your needs when you are with these full-throttle types.

❖ As for you, you want to present yourself as a happy camper with a fulfilling life. Remember that sought-after men do not want to end up with women who are waiting to be rescued.

YOUR FAMILY OF ORIGIN

A woman's family of origin is an important and vital aspect of her life: mother, father, sisters, brothers, grandparents, aunts, uncles — are all very important people. But, success with men can elude a woman who is too enmeshed with her family.

In the beginning of a new relationship, some mystery is a positive. An excellent way to mystify and de-emphasize your family is not to talk about them. The men you are dating don't really want to hear about them anyway — at least not in the beginning.

MY FAMILY	Today	Later
I rarely discuss my family with the men I date.	_____	_____
I do not include my children in my dating life.	_____	_____
Initially, I keep my family separate from the men that I date.	_____	_____
I do not show off family pictures.	_____	_____
I never mention genealogy.	_____	_____
Total	_____	_____
Divide by 5 to get your net score	_____	_____

❖ Teen age girls talk about the boys they are dating. Adult women do not discuss their personal relationships.

❖ Mature women are aware that when they become intimately involved with a man (other than their children's father), it may be traumatic for their children. Therefore, a thoughtful woman does not include her children in initial dating.

❖ A thoughtful woman informs her children that she is seeing a man that she likes. She then keeps everything concerning her children on a formal basis until the relationship is clearly defined. Only then does she bring her children into the mix.

❖ The man taking you out is courting *you*. You are not courting him.

❖ Savvy women do not invite men to meet their family or their friends until the relationship is heading toward marriage. Until that time, the men in their lives are dates, nothing more. Some women tend to jump the gun. To do so is not in their best interest.

❖ It is important to respect a man who is showing interest in you, so be careful with his confidences. Do not discuss who he is, what he does, or how much money he makes. If you do, he will resent it. Oh yes, he will know.

THE BRASS-TACKS OF CHARACTER

One indicator of character is the amount of giving a woman does for her family and community. Character is developed doing things for others with little or no thought of personal gain.

A friend of ours, named Milton, suffers from Parkinson's disease, a disease that is progressive and painful. Our friend is a good-looking, football-player type with a brilliant mind. He has a captivating smile, mesmerizing warmth and a beautiful wife who adores him. Although his physical challenges sometimes seem overwhelming, I have never heard him complain.

Milton volunteers his time helping people. In addition to the volunteer work he does, he is generous and loving with his friends. He seems to have an endless capacity for thinking of, and doing for, others. The courageous way this man lives his life is an inspiration.

Giving of oneself has a positive effect on the person doing the giving and is very appealing to others, including the opposite sex.

MY CHARACTER	Today	Later
I try to give freely of my time to charitable organizations.	_____	_____
I support worthy causes with my money.	_____	_____
I am available when a family member or friend needs me.	_____	_____
I try to keep the spotlight pointed away from myself.	_____	_____
I strive to be absolutely trustworthy. I behave ethically, even with very difficult people.	_____	_____
Total	_____	_____
Divide by 5 to get your net score	_____	_____

❖ Character is developed when we engage in giving of our time and talent.

❖ Sharing one's money is also a character builder.

❖ Being available to family members is yet another way of giving.

FINAL SCORE CARD | Today | Later

	Today	Later
Personal Hygiene	_____	_____
Dress Code	_____	_____
Listening Skills	_____	_____
Speech Patterns	_____	_____
Home	_____	_____
Money	_____	_____
Friendships	_____	_____
Alcohol	_____	_____
Weight	_____	_____
Driving Habits	_____	_____
Career	_____	_____
Family of Origin	_____	_____
Character	_____	_____
YOUR FINAL SCORE	_____	_____

If you have 39 or more, give yourself an A.

If you have between 26 and 38, give yourself a B.

If you have between 13 and 25, give yourself a C.

If you have less than 13, give yourself a D.

If you got an A, good for you, but don't stop now.

If you got a B, you are in good shape, but you have areas that need attention.

If you got a C, you have work to do, but make your changes and watch your life improve.

If you got a D, you are probably being too hard on yourself.

Nothing in the world can take the place of persistence.

Talent will not; nothing is more common than unsuccessful men with talent.

Genius will not; un-rewarded genius is almost a proverb.

Education will not. The world is full of educated derelicts.

Persistence and determination alone are omnipotent.

Calvin Coolidge

Sex is Not a Recreational Drug

I n today's world casual sex is almost a given, but women who have 'been there' and 'done that' are now beginning to long for something more. Women are deciding that getting to know you does not have to mean needing to show you.

The women who are more cautious about surrendering sexually do not get as seriously hurt as their more easy-going sisters. Therefore, it is safe to assume that women who are being hurt by men are doing something that is *not* in their best interest. Until women are willing to consider the possibility of initially withholding sex, nothing much will change.

You can't trust him until you have tested him.

So, how does a woman who has been hurt once too often, convince herself to surrender sexually?

Women who have been seriously hurt must come to realize that sexual intercourse is similar to nuclear energy. It must be intelligently regulated. Unfortunately, women who continue to *do* what they have been doing, will continue to *get* what they have been getting.

The best way to facilitate future sexual surrender is to postpone intimate sexual activity until you are positive that the man in your life cares about you. Once you can trust his sincerity, sexual surrender comes more naturally. Being certain of a man's intentions before saying "yes" is the way of taking better care of you

If "no" drives him away, he wasn't really interested.

Noteworthy men who have succeeded in the world are no longer driven solely by their hormones. Dynamic men who are in a position to choose want women who are capable of sexual surrender. If saying "no" drives a man away, he was not interested in you in the first place.

"IT'S NOBODY'S BUSINESS BUT MINE"

Years ago, while I was having coffee with a highly successful actress who is extraordinarily beautiful, she stopped me in mid-sentence and said with conviction,

"Jade! What I do in the privacy of my own home is nobody's business but my own." She then went on to say that as far as she was concerned, sex was no big deal.

"When I'm horny, I find some good-looking stud, get it on and then get back to my life."

Sounds great doesn't it? But years later, this stunningly beautiful and nationally acclaimed woman is still single and very much alone. Women still envy her, but she definitely is not married…and may never be.

THE HIGH COST OF CASUAL SEX

Let's talk more about sex. Have you ever had sex on a first date? Have you ever said "yes" to sex and later wished you had said "no"?

As I have said, women who can successfully engage in casual sex have learned how to suppress their natural instincts, and have developed strong emotional defenses. Over time, their defense mechanisms create a hardness that shows up on their faces and is evidenced in their demeanor. And, we all know women who have *that look*. Paradoxically, women who recognize the look in others often do not see it in themselves.

Casual sex too often causes pain and suffering. If you are dreaming of a satisfying life with a good man, you will be wise to consider allowing some time to elapse before engaging in sexual intercourse. If you can hold off, you will wind up with a more devoted life-partner.

You may be thinking this book has no value for you. Especially if over the years you have learned to control your emotional responses to the degree that you are able to be free spirited and cavalier about sex. But even for women who have developed impressive emotional control, casual sex can still bring excruciating heart break.

As I keep saying, in order for a woman to engage in casual sex, she must wall herself off from her natural emotions. If you have become adept at doing this, you may eventually find it difficult to *surrender* when the right man does come along.

The defense mechanisms that keep you emotionally safe enough to engage in casual sex also effect vulnerability. Additionally, having sexual intercourse without emotional connection can become a habit that is difficult to break.

SEXUAL IDENTIFICATION CARD

Imagine if you will that in the future every woman in the United States is required by law to carry a Sexual Identification Card. This card would list all of your past sexual experiences. Every time a man invites you to have dinner with him, you would be required by law to show your S.I.D.

How would you feel about showing such a card to the next man you wanted to impress? Would you feel proud? Would you feel ashamed? Would you be defensive?

Are you aware that it is usually impossible to hide promiscuity from men?

ONE WOMAN'S ANSWER TO LONELINESS

I am reminded of a stunning blond who had been taking full advantage of the sexual revolution. Maria, not her real name, was born into a family of privilege.

As an adult, she founded her own business and became internationally known in the field of art. She was a professionally successful woman.

In the early nineties, while attending an A-list party, she noticed a handsome man trying to get her attention. When she smiled

She changed into something more comfortable.

back at him, he crossed the room, as on command. They talked and laughed and then, without a second thought, she invited him back to her Beverly Hills apartment.

When she finished showing off her art collection – the pseudo reason for inviting him in the first place – she casually said, "Wait a minute while I change into something more comfortable."

He smiled! She smiled! She slyly disappeared into her bedroom, closing the door behind her.

As she began shedding pantyhose and black stretch pants, she suddenly remembered that her purse was lying on the coffee table. This purse not only contained her credit cards and a good deal of cash, but also some very expensive jewelry.

"What should I do?" she thought. "Shall I make up an excuse and go back into the living room and retrieve my purse?"

After all, she didn't really know this man. What if? What if?

As she slumped on the side of her bed, she suddenly thought, "My God, Maria, you think more of your purse than you do of your body."

Find the truth earlier — rather than later.

Taking a few minutes to get her breathing under control, she returned to the living room, after first throwing on her robe and tying it tightly.

She gave her male guest a barefoot tour of the rest of her art collection, said how delighted she was to have met him, and guided him out the front door, shutting it in his rather startled face.

IF YOU SAY NO — MEAN NO

Because men are competitive, they challenge, they argue, they try to convince women that their need for immediate sexual fulfillment is an imperative. To better protect yourself from their aggressive behavior, why not become more proactive?

Say what you mean and mean what you say. Then if necessary say it again. When...

He says:	I love you and I want you.
You say:	I'm not ready to have sex yet.
He says:	If you cared about me, you would want me as much as I want you.
You repeat:	I do care about you, but I'm just not ready yet.
He insists:	But I want you so desperately.
You repeat:	I know, but I'm not ready.

It isn't necessary to argue and you don't have to stomp your foot and get mad. You simply state your case...and then repeat yourself. Remember that "I" statements do not require an explanation. Men of value will respect your position.

A man without integrity will imply that giving in to his biological need is necessary for continuation of the relationship. If this happens, put on your jogging shoes and run for your life! God knows, you don't need one more round with another loser.

RELEGATED TO A CASUAL CATEGORY

Sometimes when men lose interest, they put women in a "casual" category, but continue to see them. In other words, they continue to see the woman for sex! Women who get caught in these selfish liaisons get hurt!

When a woman permits personal disregard, men react with even more negligence. Being discounted in such a way increases the woman's inadequacy and makes it even more difficult for her to say "no" the next time.

GIVING UP SEX....FOR A WHILE

Those few women who have not been hurt by men are easily able to surrender sexually. But for most women, sexual surrender is difficult.

If you are a woman who has had one too many sexual encounters (and most women have) and you want to get your life back on track, one way to repair the emotional damage that has resulted from unhappy sexual experiences is abstinence. Six months of not dating (your decision) and a more vibrant you will appear.

Does the thought of sexual abstinence sound impossible? Consider this: The minute a woman stops having sex, she stops having relationship failures. When a woman stops getting hurt by men, her self-esteem returns. Once self-esteem returns, she becomes less defensive. And then, more desirable and worthwhile men will be attracted to her. Temporary abstinence works.

CINDY MADE A BAD CHOICE

She was an attractive divorcee who had never been very successful with men. When she turned forty, she got a job with a large advertising firm.

From day one, her boss who was very attractive, rich and married began paying attention to her.

Several weeks after starting the new job, the boss invited Cindy to join him for an evening at the Music Center. He explained that although he was married, he and his wife had a non-marriage.

Unfortunately, Cindy said yes.

"Before the concert, he took me to an elegant restaurant for dinner," she said. "He was so attentive, that at one point, I actually thought I was going to faint.

"At the end of the evening, I invited him up for a nightcap and we made love.

"The next day at work, I couldn't believe it when he all but ignored me. At first I was crushed, but then it dawned on me that he was ignoring me because we were at work. I was positive he would call as soon as I got home.

"But he did not!

"The following day, this man who had made such passionate love to me continued to be indifferent. By the end of the week, he was still treating me like I didn't exist.

"I was so heartbroken that I quit my job."

This is such a sad story. Unfortunately, it is all too familiar.

DECISIONS HAVE TO BE MADE

I am not naïve enough to think women can just say "no" and casually walk away from long-term sexual relationships. Please!

What should a woman do when she finds herself in the middle of a long-standing sexual relationship that is going nowhere? The first thing she should do is ask herself some questions: Do I really want to spend the rest of my life with this man? Or am I seeing him only for sex?

It is important to get honest with one's self. If you decide that you are in love and want to spend the rest of your life with him, you need to think about why the relationship isn't moving forward, and ask yourself what *you* have been doing that isn't working.

If you are *not* in love with the man you are dating, you need to ask yourself why you are wasting your time.

Either way, *you* need to take action.

Some women enter into romantic relationships with very few skills and get hurt over and over again. One of the biggest mistakes women make is thinking they have rights. They call men on the phone— we're supposed to be equals aren't we? —they send e-mails, invite men to things, buy gifts, and offer to drive half way. As a result of their attitude, they also argue, cajole and try to control. This seldom works!

Today's women have been influenced by the feminist movement, which encourages and challenges women to get their fair share. This is all well and good in business, but it doesn't work well in intimate relationships with achieving men. I learned this the hard way.

WOMEN HAVE TO CHOOSE

Women have very different standards when it comes to men. For some women financial security is of the utmost importance. For other women romantic love is the top priority.

Consider the following two types of men. Which is more descriptive of the man you dream of finding?

Mr. Romantic

Smooth and self-assured

Masculine and sexy

Unusually vulnerable

A skilled lover

Socially polished

Loves to play

Loves to flirt

Dresses casually

May be spoiled and willful

Mr. Accomplished

Strong and in charge

A leader

Sometimes self-absorbed

Good in bed but not a 10

Politically active

Loves to work

Does not openly flirt

Dresses carefully

Is probably ultra-responsible

If you have chosen Mr. Romantic, he may not be a great wage earner, but life with him will be vibrant and exciting. On the other hand, you could experience disappointment when you see other women enjoying advantages that you do not have.

If you have chosen Mr. Accomplished, he may not be as fun-loving as you would like. He will, however, provide you with life's luxuries. But you may find yourself longing for more attention than he is able to provide. And there could be times when you envy your girl friend who seems to be having more fun.

The man in your life will be much like you.

If your choice is Mr. Romantic, you too must be easy going and fun loving. If your choice is Mr. Accomplished, you must be hard working and responsible. One thing is for sure: the man with whom you end up will be a mirror reflection of you. There is no more accurate way of knowing who you are than by taking an honest look at the man you are seeing regularly.

SAY HELLO TO THE NO! CHART

I was involved in a disastrous love affair. When it ended, I felt worthless. I was certain no significant man would ever be interested in me again.

A friend, after patiently listening to me for days, suggested that I begin a No Chart. She assured me that the quality of men asking me out would improve if I was conscientious about keeping it.

Only *after* you are married should your focus shift to him.

She forgot to tell me how long it would take. It took nine months.

I was told to print the word NO in big letters at the top of a piece of paper. I was to tack this paper to the inside of my closet door and every time some less-than-desirable man asked me out, I was to write his name (or description) on my chart.

I did as instructed.

After several months, I began noticing something very strange. Every time I said no to a man, the *next* man to ask me out was of a slightly higher caliber than the one before him.

There were nine names on my No Chart when my now husband asked me to marry him.

NO!

- ❖ The young muscle-man at the car wash who suggested we get together sometime.

- ❖ That aggressive shoe salesman who flirted with me while I was buying a pair of shoes for my daughter. (He had the nerve to ask for my phone number.)

- ❖ The stockroom clerk who invited me to have lunch with him, and asked me if I would mind driving my car.

- ❖ An electrical engineer who suggested we get-it-on sometime.

- ❖ My ex-husband's best friend who invited me to have dinner with him, but cautioned me not to mention this to either his wife or my ex-husband.

- ❖ The law partner who insisted upon drawing up a legal document for me 'free of charge' and suggested I meet him at the Ritz Carlton so he could properly witness my signature.

- ❖ The L.A. Deputy District Attorney who told me he was falling in love with me, and explained that he wasn't really married. (His wife was confined to a sanitarium.)

- ❖ The big-time corporate executive who invited me to go to Africa on a Shooting Safari, carefully explaining that we would shop for my clothes and rifle after we arrived in Nairobi. (This "no" was a hard one.)

- ❖ The suave and so good-looking (married) mid-level executive who worked in my to-be husband's company, who asked me to go to Palm Springs with him for the weekend.

After the end of my tortuous love affair, my walk toward matrimonial bliss felt like an endless crawl through a dark tunnel.

The men who came into my life began with a car-wash attendant and slowly proceeded to a mid-level executive.

However, by the time the mid-level executive suggested I go with him to Palm Springs for the weekend, my self-esteem had returned! I was no longer a broken little waif. I had acquired some self-esteem once again. I remember smiling at this jerk and saying, "No, thank you. I'm fishing for marlin!"

Then, feeling sufficiently acquitted, I remember holding my head high, putting my shoulders back and sauntering out of the office. This was the beginning of the life I have today.

Four months later, I ran into this letch on the company elevator. But things were very different now. I was sporting a gorgeous four-carat diamond ring.

"I see you caught your Marlin," he sneered.

I smiled. I didn't say a word because I didn't have to. We both knew that I was getting ready to marry *his* boss.

THE DO'S AND DON'TS

This is an important section! If you read carefully, the suggestions in this section will help you develop into the kind of woman that captures the interest of high caliber men.

Keep in mind that the more successful the man, the more he will initially expect to control of the relationship. Career-successful women must be very careful not to 'take over' while they are being courted. Extra discipline is required if an assertive woman hopes to capture the heart of a top-flight man.

DO NOT

Do not call men on the telephone.

They will call you when they are ready.

Do not agree to meet men.

They should be picking you up.

Do not run errands for or with men you are dating.

They wouldn't ask an esteemed colleague to run errands with them.

Do not accept last minute invitations – to anything.

No matter how much you might want to.

Do not discuss your family or your friends.

In the beginning, they are only interested in you.

They are not interested in your relatives and friends.

Do not offer to drive your car.

You are his guest.

Do not try to take charge of the relationship.

Allow him that privilege.

Do not discuss other men. Never do this!

Neither praise nor condemn other men, especially past husbands or boyfriends.

Do not accept expensive gifts from men.

This creates a sense of obligation on your part and expectation on his.

Do not compliment the new man in your life.

He should be complimenting you. Your show of too much appreciation of him may be seen as cloying.

Do not discuss your health.

He is not your doctor.

Do not talk about your problems.

He is not your psychiatrist.

He is not looking for a neurotic in need of his emotional support.

Do not allude to the future.

Keep your fantasies to yourself.

Do not offer to pay – for anything.

It is way too soon to share financial responsibilities with him.

Do not talk about your children.

He is not yet interested in them — even if he asks questions.

He needs to establish his interest in you first.

Do not allow his children (or yours) on your dates.

This is a time to decide if you want to move forward.

Don't allow children to interfere with your judgment.

Do not talk to him on the phone for long periods of time.

Supposedly your life is busy.

Do not invite him to your family social events.

> He is not yet your husband or your fiancé. Keep it simple in the beginning.

Do not go on overnight trips with him.

> Not unless you have a real commitment or have given up on marriage.

Do not ask, "Are you going to call me?"

> He will call when he wants to — without prompting.

Do not ask, "When will I see you again?"

> He will ask to see you again when he decides to.

> Pressuring men scares them off.

> Only needy women ask this kind of question.

Do not make assumptions.

> You are only a guest.

> The future is yet to be decided.

> The first moves are his to make.

Do not leap into bed with him at your first opportunity.

> Make sure your first sexual experience is something special.

> Wait until he is in love with you and has made a commitment.

DO

Do insist upon being treated with respect.

Leave if he is disrespectful.

Do act like a guest since that is what you are.

It will encourage him to treat you with more respect.

Do keep your own counsel.

He will be delighted not to be involved in your affairs.

Do stay closely connected to your friends and family.

Don't cancel plans with them to be with him!

He needs to understand that you have a full life.

Do continue to concentrate on your responsibilities.

He will be favorably impressed.

Do remember that your children need you.

Continue to give your children the attention they deserve.

He will be impressed.

Too often a woman abandons her friends and family when she becomes obsessed with a new man. This is one of the dumbest things a woman can do. Men are not intrigued by women who give up their personal lives before they have been asked to do so.

I urge you to stay actively involved in your own life until after he has made a serious commitment to you. To do otherwise is to risk losing your friends and your family as well as the man himself.

To keep this undesirable characteristic from showing its ugly head, you must have a satisfying life of your own.

If you are hoping to find a man who will rescue you, men sense it and successful men will run for their lives.

Remember that every time you pick up the telephone and call a man you are demonstrating your neediness. You are also giving away 80% of your power.

DON'T FORGET

If the man you are seeing has come back more than twice—and you haven't yet had sex—marriage is a definite possibility.

At this point in time, there are five steps that—if you follow them—will almost guarantee success. 1) Do not chase him. 2) Focus on your own life. 3) Become a very good listener. 4) Save sex until after you have a commitment. 5) Keep uppermost in mind that you are his guest.

Magic steps that lead to the altar.

Regardless of how often a man tells you that he likes hearing from you, never phone him. And don't forget that the man you are dating will never again be as willing to please you as he is on your first few dates. Smart women know the significance of first encounters. They approach first dates the same way they approach important job interviews.

Truly sophisticated women know to ask intelligent questions and stay focused on their date. They never talk about themselves. In other words, women-in-the-know are intent on making a good first impression.

I hope you are now more aware of the importance of establishing firm boundaries. And I want to re-emphasize that non-verbal communication is one of the most effective, and least offensive, way of getting your needs met.

Your first few dates are crucial.

Remember that desirable men are being pursued by scores of eager women, and most of these women will be making mistakes that you will not be making. These mistakes include: calling men on the phone, being available at the last minute, agreeing to meet men half-way, picking up part of the tab, cooking intimate dinners, running errands with and for him, and saying "yes" too soon.

You will stand out from other women if you resist.

Men with high levels of testosterone—and aren't these the men women want?—they love to compete and pursue, so let them.

Remember: You are *not* his psychologist. You are *not* his housekeeper. You are *not* his babysitter. You are *not* his chauffeur. You are *not* his executive assistant.

Lastly, I urge you to go very slowly into your next sexual relationship. I caution you not to trust too soon.

The man you are dating is not your best friend. Nor does he become your best friend until after he has asked you to become his wife.

A Love Story

The following story is my favorite. I hope it will warm your heart the way it does mine.

Barbara lost her husband to cancer after a fifteen-year marriage. They had been very close and she was grief-stricken without him. For months, she did nothing but cry.

Eventually she realized she had to get back into life, so she started dating. But after several blind dates, including one man she had known for years, she quit dating altogether.

She told me that the thought of going on yet another date made her sick to her stomach. She wanted to concentrate on her own life. Barbara got busy and redecorated her house. She returned to playing golf. She volunteered one day a week at a local hospital. She lunched with friends.

She had hoped that staying busy would assuage her grief. It did not.

One day, in the middle of what seemed to her like a never-ending nightmare, she remembered that as a little girl she had loved fly-fishing with her father.

With a kind of last-minute desperation, she called UCLA and was told there was an Extension course for fly-fishing. (Yes, UCLA Extension did indeed offer a course in fly-fishing.)

Barbara enrolled.

The first day of class, the instructor announced that at the end of the quarter, there would be a three-day field trip up into the San Bernardino Mountains.

"How nice," Barbara thought.

On the second day of class, an attractive man to whom Barbara had never spoken, walked purposefully across the room and sat down in the seat next to her.

"He started talking to me," she told me.

"I could tell he was interested, but I really meant it when I said no more men."

Thereafter, Barbara made a point of staying as far away from this aggressive stranger as possible. She went out of her way to completely ignore him.

"I knew I was being rude, but I just couldn't help myself," she said.

But Barbara found that she thoroughly enjoyed the fly-fishing class. She quickly made friends with the other women in the class, and began looking forward to the upcoming field trip.

At the end of the quarter, the instructor did indeed charter a bus and the entire class went fishing.

My friend was in seventh heaven.

On the last day of the fishing trip, the man who had been so aggressively friendly at the beginning of the quarter, walked over to the spot where Barbara was fishing and cast his line next to hers.

This annoyed my friend terribly because she was thoroughly enjoying her solitude.

She told me later that she contemplated moving away, but for some reason changed her mind. After fishing beside her in silence for almost an hour, the man finally began a conversation.

To her own surprise, Barbara found herself enjoying talking with him. Before the day was over, she was even considering the possibility that they might become friends.

Six weeks later they were married!

I think my friend's love story is delicious. It is even more romantic and exciting because her new husband is a very prominent physician.

Barbara asked her new husband why he had chosen her, out of all of women who seemed to be so interested in him. She beamed as she shared his answer with me.

"At first I was intrigued because you didn't pester me," he said. "I guess I found you challenging because of your seeming indifference. But, it wasn't until the last day of the fishing trip that I realized I wanted you by my side for the rest of my life."

THE END

I would like to thank my friend Larry MacDonald for his endless patience and skillful guidance.

I also want to thank four friends: Win Weaver, Joy Hayward, Andrea Rock and Patricia Haight for their considerable efforts on my behalf.

I am grateful to my sister-in-law Marian Rollin for her painstaking editing.

And my love always to my husband for his devotion and constant support.

Jade Brode has spent years counseling upwardly-mobile women in the entertainment industry and the business world who were successful in their chosen careers, but failing to attract men of value.

The dynamic women she worked with were becoming more and more despondent as they watched the clock ticking away, knowing they were not even succeeding with men of lesser value. They credit Jade's counseling style with changing their lives.

Jade lives in Southern California with her husband, a strategic missiles scientist.